Imaginary Lines

Stories of Physical, Cultural and Culinary Frontiers

Linton Robinson
and
Ana Maria Corona

Copyright © 2008 By Linton Robinson
First Edition

1. Literature. 2. Short Stories. 3. Fiction - General.

Imaginary Lines: Stories of Physical, Cultural, and Culinary Frontiers
/ by   Linton Robinson
p. cm.

ISBN 13: 978-0-9721349-9-9

adorobooks.com

In Collaboration with Bauu Press
Boulder, Colorado

Printed in the United States of America
ALL RIGHTS RESERVED

In loving memory of

Tañia Luisa Rodriguez Corona

About the Book . . .

All stories in this book were previously published in the San Diego *Reader*, with these exceptions: "Cradle of Wolves" appeared in the late, lamented *Baja Week*, portions of "Flowers In The Dust" appeared in *Harpers*. "Faith, Aphrodisiacs, and Freeze-Dried Blood" was commissioned by the *Reader*, but never paid for.

- L.R.

Imaginary Lines

Stories of Physical, Cultural and Culinary Frontiers

Linton Robinson
and
Ana Maria Corona

CONTENTS

I. WATER FOR CHOCOLATE, MILK FOR COLUMBUS

The English translation of Laura Esquivel's book *Como Agua Para Chocolate* appeared in San Diego at the same time the film version premiered in Tijuana. Readers of English liked the book and it achieved the bestseller list, but the impact of the film in Mexico was still stronger: it was the film of the year. Everyone saw it, everyone loved it. Much more than *Danzon* (for all the Ariel awards it won), *Como Agua* is making people believe that Mexican cinema has not died nor become capable only of mafioso massacres and bosom comedies. The coincidence of the English book and Mexican film presenting at the same time across the border is, to me, much like the coincidence of both book and film appearing at the time of the Five Hundred year commemoration of the opening of the new world by Europeans. That is my private view, but I will try to demonstrate it to you in my own way.

The story is of Tita, who falls in love with Pedro. But since she is the youngest daughter in the family, tradition says she must not marry, but stay in the home to care for her mother in her old age; Tita's mother refuses Pedro her hand. Love finds a way; Pedro marries Tita's sister so he can be near her. The way that Tita finds love is cooking for her loved one. The ultimate expression of that impulse comes toward the end of the film, when Tita suckles the child of her sister and the

11

man she loves on her own virginal breasts that suddenly run with mother's milk. There are those who see this as fantasy, as a sort of literary magic trick. Actually, it is merely a mystery. Magic is merely ritual, mysteries are merely secrets.

A noted novelty of *Como Agua Para Chocolate* is that each chapter opens with a recipe. Neither is this a trick nor gimmick, it expresses the integral nature of food and its preparation into the life of families. These are far more than recipes like those bought in magazines. A writer could publish a recipe for making a cup of Japanese tea, but most readers know there is ceremony far beyond measures and movements. People are aware of the Japanese ritual of making tea because it is so stylized and set apart from normal cooking and drinking. Mexican cooking contains rituals just as elaborate, depending just as much on concentration and inner sensation, but contained in the quotidian world of feeding the bodily appetite. Even a simple *mole* sauce can involve selecting a dozen *chiles* and grinding them on stones until they are judged finished by touch, texture and smell. Even making tortillas can be a deep and lengthy rite, a handcraft.

In one major scene in the film, Tita has to bake the wedding cake for her sister's marriage feast. Her tears fall into the food she's preparing, an additional ingredient the cameras catch and show us. That added human salt could serve as a symbol of another unlisted ingredient we often ignore; the love and giving-ness of the one who prepares it, perhaps something to do with the "salt of the earth".

With all our scientific knowledge about calories and amino acids, modern Western culture still overlooks the heart and soul of food. Mexico should be included in the modern West because we like to think of ourselves that way and because we ignore the ways of our native races as firmly as countries where the European races are purer and the indigenous ones more reduced. This concept of the nutritive importance of love has been reduced to a quaint wive's fable, an unproven fad like eating zinc or laetrile or acidophilus.

It is like the statements on American vitamin supplements: *No Daily Minimum. Nutritional Need Not Established.* George Ohsawa, whose Macrobiotics theories were internationally influential in the nineteen sixties, stated it directly: it is only the amount of love in food that sustains us, that all the chemicals are details and illusions. We survive on factory food, Ohsawa would say, only because it contains the love of the plants and sun. Now his work is regarded as another diet fad, a curiosity. That need is not numbered by science but neither is it unknown: only when it is stated as a prose fact, does it becomes folkloric like flying saucers, astrology, or cholesterol.

Speaking of the Japanese, Americans seem to think of them as being more in tune with nature while Mexicans think of them as a form of "supergringo"; even more efficient, materialistic and synthetic. We may admire the simplicity and purity of their cuisine, but we buy their processed noodles in chemical sauces, their super-instant MSG soups. Yet the Japanese film, *Tampopo*, which was a huge popular success among the universities and art communities in many large Mexican cities, made that same point very clearly.

In that way it is a film very much like *Como Aqua Para Chocolate*. In one scene a mother rises from her deathbed to prepare one last meal for her family and the doctor, then dies with a happy smile. Yet that message is hidden, has to be pulled out in a secret hunt through the industrialized, fast-train world of modern Japan, a world not very different from Mexico City or Los Angeles. When men tell us these kinds of truth, we don't often believe them; these are women's secrets that bind the world together. Even as it falls apart. Know what you are eating, who to thank for it. . . is that really such a secret?

Some of my most vivid memories from childhood are of my grandparents' ranch, several hours drive from Guadalajara, near a little Jalisco highlands town called Tepatitlan. It was an old house of the end-of-the-century Porfirio Diaz period before the Revolution, a central patio sur-

13

rounded by arched corridors and high-roofed rooms. I loved the old house with its dull yellow and red paint, full-length barred windows with slatted shutters, and patio full of potted plants. It seemed full of quiet, soft mysteries to us girls.

We weren't allowed into the front parlor, a French salon typical of the *Porfiriato* style, but we would stare into it and wonder at the ornate furniture and the walls hung with a century of family relics. Dozens of massive metal frames with stiff brown photographs of stiff brown people in stiff brown suits; women holding nameless children and old men holding swords or rifles. There were no men working in fields or women in kitchens. We got tours of the parlor at times, so I knew that the proud young railroad man with a huge curled mustache was really my grandfather, Amado Corona. The portrait of my grandmother, Primavera Espinosa, was anonymous, a very typical young woman waiting for a man and children to mold her body and character.

The high interiors of the Tepatitlan house were lowered by hanging thin fabric ceilings painted in various styles of folk art, even ornamental church art. The false ceiling in my room looked to me like the Sistine chapel, a marvel out of history. That bedroom was like a ship into another world. The place was a wonderland of secrets; nothing there was done in the same way as in the outer world. The beds were so high we felt tiny and had to jump onto them and wiggle into the thick covers.

We giggled at the white enamel pans under the beds, but none of us would have wanted to go outside at night to use the primitive outhouse. We could wash in our bedrooms because there were wrought iron stands holding huge enamel basins painted with *Talavera* patterns, big pitchers of fresh water, and thick white cotton towels. I always left a little water in the pitcher since whoever emptied it had to go out into the patio and fill it from the well. I liked watching the bucket drop down the brick well, but pulling it back up with the rope was hard work. One secret I discovered was that my older sisters, Magnolia and Jacaranda, often crept into my room to use the bedpan so they wouldn't have to empty the one in their room.

The kitchen was long and painted brick red. When it was empty, it looked quiet and solemn like a civic square, but during cooking and meals, it became a red, pulsing heart of the house. A counter ran down one wall, so high that I was in school before I could see what was on top without standing on my toes or a stool. In the counter was a stove like a big barbecue that burned wood my grandfather cut with an ax and brought into the patio. Part of the stove was a ceramic grill, part was metal for making *carne asada*. There were bowls and big clay jugs of water, but all the washing was done outside in a stone sink. Vegetables were kept fresh in a cupboard of screen shelves. There was a huge wooden table where we ate all our meals. Baskets woven of palm fronds hung from the ceiling and walls, full of spices and bread loaves. I liked the *jarritos* on the wall; little clay jars hanging from nails in arched rows to make a pattern like a rainbow.

My grandmother's cooking was wonderful; rich enough to make my parents and cousins laugh and beat on the table and rain compliments, strong enough to impress even city children with tastes formed by candies and restaurants and street cooking. But it wasn't the food that intrigued me most, it was the plenitude and rawness of it, the way it was stored in great fresh piles. I especially loved the pantry outside the kitchen. It was heaped with rough cloth sacks of grains, and hung to the roof were ropes of garlic, strings of brown sausages and hams, and huge masses of drying *chiles*. I would go in there and look at all that food hanging from the *vigas* that supported the roof. Then I would close the door and lay in the dark on sacks of corn, trying to isolate and identify the various smells that filled the place. There was a special heat in that room. It might have come from the *chiles* themselves, but I assumed it was a sort of magic, a mystery I associated with my grandmother. I wanted to know it, make it mine.

15

My grandmother would rise from her bed every morning at four to allow time to make the tortillas for the day. Sometimes she would wake one of us, or maybe one of the older girls to bring down one of the small girls, and we would see how tortillas were made. I came to think of my parents as old-fashioned, but I never saw my grandmother as anything other than classical, timeless. She was old when I first saw her and never got older until suddenly she was no longer alive.

That kitchen was a niche carved out of time for me and I would sit on the counter sleepy, almost dreaming, to watch her work. She set Spanish silverware at the table, but used the same kitchen utensils as the Aztecs; grinding fresh chiles into salsa in a three-legged *molcajete* of black volcanic stone or grinding meat and corn and chocolate on a *metate* of the same rough rock, so old that the tapered stone *metlapil* had worn the hard basalt to conform to its shape.

In that room, in that house, standing straight and calm in her black clothes that covered all of her but her face and hands, her thick silver hair falling straight to her waist, she could have been a woman of the late fifteenth century, when Guadalajara was established. Her hands could have been ancient, moving the old stones in patterns of centuries. I would nod sleepily and watch her as if in a dream. She didn't talk about what she was doing, but I saw everything she did. I can close my eyes and see it now as I sit and write this.

Not that I enjoyed that education so much. I would rather have been sleeping. It was grueling work to make a tortilla the way she did, and I think you'd agree that the celebrated Japanese tea ritual was nothing to compare to it. She had rasped the corn off the cob days before, using a handful of dried corncobs lashed together into a very rough scrubbing tool. She had soaked the corn grains in water overnight to soften them, then boiled them with lime to make *nixtamal*, the basic mix. She had already rubbed the *nixtamal* mixture on the stone washboard outside by hand to remove the outer shell of the corn.

So, in the hours before dawn she would work by lantern light, using a hand-cranked metal mill to grind the scrubbed corn into *masa*, or dough. The grinding had to be steady, with pressure judged by constant attention. By that time, after hours of work, she had the same kind of *masa* you can buy in any store.

But the *masa* was not fine enough, so she would mill it with water on the *metate* until it had the right consistency to her hand. Then she would roll small balls and wet her hands so they would not stick as she quickly patted them into tortillas. The quick patting motion of her hands, repeated for dozens of tortillas, would hypnotize me. My drowsy dream would close down to a circle lit by flame and my grandmother's hands touching the stone, then the water, then flashing in a circular dance.

Then she would test the heat of the *comal*, a round clay grill for cooking the tortillas. She would drop them and I would turn them, sometimes letting one burn too black. She would say, "Never mind, Anita. I'll eat that one." As the tortillas were cooked, she would put them in a round straw *tortillera* and cover them with a clean white napkin that she had embroidered with flowers and butterflies. Then the tortillas would be ready to eat.

While she prepared the tortillas she was also making breakfast for as many as were in the house. She would fry fresh Serrano *chiles* in pork lard, then take them out so the lard would carry the flavor into the refried beans. Maybe she would even melt some of her homemade soft-ripened *panela* over them. She would grind small green tomatoes in the *molcajete* and pour them over the eggs. And, best of all, she would set aside some of the corn *masa* to make *atole*, a hot Mexican breakfast drink since pre-Columbian times. Best was when she ground bitter chocolate and mixed it into the corn, milk, and boiling water to make *champurrado*. By sunrise the smell of hot chocolate would be all through the house and we would start sticking our noses out from under the big coverlets and sniffing, ready to get up. The expression *"como agua para chocolate"* is a Mexican idiom that means "ready" or "fired up". By the time we all filed in to breakfast, she'd been up for four hours, as she had six days a week her whole married life.

But by the time I was old enough to marry I had changed. You might think it strange that I would marry my first boyfriend, and that I would think of it as natural. Or at least inevitable. That was the way it was done. My older sisters had married, it was my time, the son of my father's friend was calling on me, and I was ready to have my own home. I can only say that this system worked more often than not.

I was very modern, collecting electrical appliances. I thought it was ridiculous to stand and pat dough into tortillas by hand, or even press them out one by one in a press. In fact, I didn't know how. Not only were handmade tortillas considered a mark of Indian peasant backwardness, I preferred the product of the *tortillaria*, machine-rolled and government subsidized. I had liked the machines when I first saw them as a girl. Even sweating in line for two hours in my dark Catholic school uniform I admired the way the machines methodically flattened out the dough with the measured movements of gears and rollers.

I inherited that love of machinery from my father and passed it to my daughters, who often spend their Saturdays tinkering with their tape recorders or in blue jeans under the motor of their faulty Toyota. I think it was the first time that I saw my oldest daughter Nayeli with a water pump in her greasy hands that I wondered, if this really was progress. Nayeli, do I need to say, would not know how to make water for chocolate without burning it.

I remember my grandmother standing for hours in the half-light of the old rust-red kitchen, rotating the rolls of corn paste between her hands as she patted them into flat discs for cooking. My mother bought prepared flour and used a small aluminum press to squeeze out tortillas. I buy them premade from the grocery outlet on L Street in Chula Vista where I cross the border each week to shop. I always hate to disappoint foreign readers who like to picture Mexicans living in adobe huts and enjoying a hearty life of rich soil and gay festivals. But I am a modern university woman, and single mother with car payments and credit card bills. My son wants a Nintendo. I'm trying to afford a computer. I go to the supermarket and buy what I can afford, what I have time for. It makes sense.

Until my mother comes to visit and sees my canned food and sauces and looks around to tell me, "You have no time to cook? So you are divorced and your children have no respect for you and want to leave home like American children. What important things do you do with your time?" Then I wonder. But what can I do? My sister has lived in Chula Vista for years and barely uses tortillas at all. We sometimes talk, at night in front of a fire when we are alone or with our girls, about my grandmother making tortillas. When I go into an old-fashioned market, I stop and smell the many smells. That makes sense, too. But not in a way I could put in my computer. But Laura Esquivel put it in a book, even in a film.

They say that the English version of *Como Agua Para Chocolate* will be released next year. I think it will be as popular in San Diego as it has been in Tijuana, especially with women. It is the kind of film that women like; a sad joy of spiritual love overcoming sexual impossibility, like the Australian *Thorn Birds*. It has occurred to me that Americans might find Tita's situation a little melodramatic and hard to understand. Family duty being more important than personal happiness might seem strange just as American readers probably react to the women in the Bronte sisters' books, forced by custom to await the marriage of their older sisters.

You might find it hard to accept the much crueler fate of being born into a status where marriage is denied altogether; to be born like a nun in the worship of one's own mother and family. It might be hard to realize that it was the old form of social security, before the government became mother to us all. But of course, the story comes from the last century; you would not expect such to exist today. The truth is, in the last ten years I have seen several of my friends—self sufficient college educated women living and working on their own—having to give it up and move home to take care of their parents, generally their mother.

Liggia, a pretty and fun-loving Mexico City girl in her twenties who I used to work with, passed into a depression when she heard about her brother's engagement. He was the last child living at home, so she would become the last child not married. Her mother would be left alone in the house unless she gave up her career, her friends, her men, her life at the border where she could enjoy American cinema and beaches. She would have to leave it all to go live with a very difficult woman in a bad part of a big city. She complained to us, but the pressure of family duty was too great to seriously resist. She moved back home in time for her brother's wedding and within six months married the first man who asked her.

There is this about Mexico, our traditions change very slowly. This is a weakness but also a strength, which is another major point of *Como Agua Para Chocolate*. Instead of being trapped and enslaved in the kitchen, Tita makes the kitchen a throne, feeds the past to the future, turns her chains into bonds.

Anyone would recognize in this film themes that touch on a woman's role in life, another tradition that is changing slowly. I won't say anything about matters of liberation except to ask (as we each have to ask ourselves), "What is liberation? From what? To what?" Because there are also deeper themes that might be less obvious to non-Mexicans, which returns me to my private argument about the conquest of this hemisphere. Just as Mexican cooking absorbed and overpowered Spanish cuisine, tempting traditions with new foods like *chile*, chocolate, tomatoes, and peanuts, the European conquest of Mexico turned out very differently from that of North America and Canada. Here the Europeans intermarried with native women and Mexico is a *mestizo* country bringing forth our greatest strength, our greatest weakness.

That very mixing of blood, symbolized most powerfully by the convergence of different colored blood vessels in Frida Kahlo's famous self-portrait, *Las Dos Fridas*, came from Spaniards marrying and having children by native women. From the iron crush and grinding rape came dark children and a non-European nation. You don't read about that most secret conquest because it's too obvious; the European steel machine came and ground and squeezed but what lasted were women giving up their bodies, loving their families, feeding their men, tending their gardens. . . secret, mysterious processes transformed the bitter taste of slave crops into the sweet milk of their breasts.

Just as Mexicans once denied their Indian blood, it is fashionable today to denigrate the Spanish, to make a villain of Columbus. Fashionable or not, it is an equally bad idea: Mexicans of any heritage are Mexicans, just as whites and blacks in Los Angeles have more in common than either have with Africans or Europeans. Trying to cast off the past is ultimately as futile as trying to hold onto it. Now we want to feed off the older generation, then go off and leave them on their own, hurry on with our lives. But we leave something of ourselves; we become insubstantial as we rid ourselves of secrets and obligations. We lose the rites and turn out only to have recipes. . . mere words written down on paper. No wonder we are confused and lose sight of who we are. There's one very simple answer to that one. We are what we eat.

II. FOR LOVE NOR MONEY

I was born a peasant in a remote *rancho* in Guerrero, one of Mexico's wildest states. My father, though he had political pretensions, was little more than an armed bandit; a highwayman. Like so many fathers, he would have wished to see me follow him into his career. . . and in a way I did, a way that might have pleased him if he'd known of it. But at fourteen I moved to Acapulco, where I became a man and very much a product of that city. I worked for several years as a fisherman, but my eyes were always for the charms of the city which, in the closing years of the World War, was becoming a "jet-set" resort as well as a smuggling, seafaring town and Mexico's answer to Las Vegas, New Orleans, and Miami all in one place.

My *patrón* had a beach-seine crew. We would loop a very long net out to sea with the launch, then haul it in on the beach to scoop up the fish. By my late teens I had developed a bronzed, powerful body with strong shoulders from pulling the nets, a deep chest from diving for oysters, and a glow of health from the outdoor life and simple diet.

I cooked cast-off fish over beach fires and slept under the boat at night so I could spend all of my earnings on flashy clothes and hair pomade to set off my build and good looks. I was a neon-dazzled, cut-rate *boulevardier* trying my fortune with the local girls, going *mano a mano* against puritanical

Indian Catholicism and doing well enough to please myself. I was quite easily pleased with myself in those days. And with good reason.

But the more I saw American women, the less I enjoyed the favors of *Mexicanas*. And once I figured out what the *taloneros* were doing, I decided I was ripe for a change in careers and started spending my nights hanging around them, learning their tricks and slang and attitudes. *Taloneros* are the young sharks you always see standing around outside Mexican night-clubs, especially those that cater to tourists. The whole institution of *taloneros* is poorly understood by foreigners. I suppose there are a few naive enough to think this pack of polished young hounds is there to be seating hosts. I was only naive enough to assume they were there to take advantage of the famously looser morals of drunken American women on vacation, though they were presumably picking up a little money somehow. Even at that age, struck blind, mute and stupid by the visions of sexually permissive blondes, I was also interested in how the men made it pay.

When I'd adopted enough of their callous urban facade to overcome my hick manners (my first lesson in being able to change my style and personality like a suit of clothing) to get a straight answer to my questions about *talonero* finances, I was amazed by the revelation, struck dumb by the bright, hard, incredible scope of it. Though it was common enough to them, with their gutter sophistication.

My status changed overnight after I rather decisively won a fight with another youth who had been tormenting me about my rough hands and back-country accent. They all acted very tough and carried knives but, in the final test, a life of lounging in nightclub doors smoking "Faros" and drinking Tequila doesn't really prepare a youngster for brawling with someone who spends his days cheating a living out of the open sea. He should also have given some thought to the fact that fishermen are as familiar with knives as alley cut-throats are.

After that I was still a bumpkin, but I was "their" bumpkin, inside that wary, brittle circle that we hoodlums and deceivers maintain. A very sleek *talonero* named Enrique, a man who became a sort of coach to my career, first answered all my questions. He said, "You think we're here for the *mondonga* don't you?" That's a local word to describe the female flower. He said, "Well, Country, I get more than any man you've ever met—nice pale, clean foreign stuff. But that's just the *pilón*, the 'gravy'. Here's how it works. . ."

He explained that tourism is a very competitive business, so everybody pays commissions and kickbacks, concepts I'd already been exposed to in the fishing industry. But not to the extent that "hooking" and "landing" dominated the commerce of bars and cabarets. It turned out that there was a little *mordida* in every drink, meal, and cover charge in town. If you were a recognized member of the "guild", you had running accounts everywhere that tourists could possible spend money, from the cliff diving to the lowest level of prostitutes.

Enrique told me, "I don't work for La Huerta; I'm just waiting for the right party. Then I attach myself to them, usually by getting them in without paying the cover charge." Cover charges are a joke in such clubs, and so are the velvet ropes used to build lines of apparently eager customers if possible, but also to stop people long enough to size them up and set them up for "hooking".

Once Enrique convinced the party (ideally a group of American women, who dote on being escorted around by handsome *Latinos)* that he was their best possible ticket to the pleasures of Acapulco he would hail a taxi—there was always a taxi waiting with motor running—and take them for a ride. The *taxista* would pay him something, of course (otherwise he would hail someone who would) but the real money came from hitting hot spots. Approaching a roped-off door where other *taloneros* waited, Enrique would explain that there was, say, a six dollar cover charge, but that due to his friendship with Pablo at the door, they would be admitted for only three dollars apiece. Later he and Pablo would split the money, since the charge was imaginary. Those "hooked" would be waved in ceremoniously and Enrique would be noted as having "landed" them. Merely catching the eye of the right person would add a percentage to your account; everything they ate, drank, or bought would be fattening you up as well. Since such groups thought nothing of spending several hundred dollars a night, even a ten percent cut was substantial money. For comparison, I had been working like a slave all day for less than a dollar.

"From the time you've set the hook," Enrique told me, "It's just a matter of how long you can keep them running around spending money. The more they drink, the better." He showed me signals that would let the bartenders know to send me drinks free of alcohol, or to make stronger ones for those I'd "hooked". Other signals could lead to other things than alcohol being put in drinks, everything from sleeping pills to laxatives to Indian herbs believed to be aphrodisiacs. Enrique cautioned me that such heavy-handed methods were to be used with caution, though much of the "job" consisted of being able to judge, monitor, and maintain the level of alcohol in a group of strangers.

Enrique taught me subtle as well as basic matters of "hooking" in tourists. "Most young guys," he told me, "can't wait to pour the *gringas* into bed by the end of the night. But is that always the best move?" There are many ways to play it depending on how long they had been in town, when they were leaving, where they were from. Using the end of the evening to suggest spending the next day at the beaches could lead to more money. It was always a fine decision whether it would be more lucrative to take one of the women to bed. It could lead to the opportunity to "land" her in every place in town for her entire stay and ravish her every night. . . or it might lead her single friends pressuring her to dump you so as not to break up the band.

As a general rule, it is better to move in on older women, but treat younger women as a tour group, being their local friend and saving any sexual conquests for the last night in town. But every situation is different and calls for judgment. Sometimes I have had those last nights extend to the enjoyment of an entire group of vacationing girls.

At first, as you might guess, I ran wild sexually, running up numbers of blond trophies at the expense of my income. Enrique smiled, applauding my success, but always reminded me that, "The work comes before the poetry, my son."

He also taught me something young bravos often ignore; that my relationships with the other *taloneros,* barkeeps, and waiters were as important as my conquests of the *gringas.* "Remember who is actually paying you, *Tijera,*" he would say. He called me after a diving bird because of my fishing background, but it also means "scissors", a sexual pun referring to the spread legs and castrating qualities of a woman. "You should do well in that respect," he said, "Those colleagues you can't charm, you can kick in the *huevos* like you did to Rogelio the night I decided it was worth trying to teach you anything." I was to remember what many of the other young men forgot: that a little competition between us was fun, but it was ultimately Us versus Them—and They had the money.

With Enrique's advice, the money I was making, and my sexual success feeding the arrogant self-confidence that is so vital to a man who preys on the weakness of women, I excelled as a rake's apprentice and had no regrets for my previous life. Some other husky hick could haul in the nets; I was after bigger, softer, and more fragrant fish. After three or four years in Acapulco I felt ready to become a journeyman, to test my fortune in other areas. I had developed my own style by then, learning to do my initial "hooking" on the beaches in front of the hotels, where I could use my physique and dark bronze coloration to maximum advantage. This seemed radical and impractical to Enrique when I told him, but when I explained that I could often attach myself to tourists right at their hotels before anyone else had a chance at them (learning to judge their time in town by the color of their skin), he nodded his head in appreciation and told me he had nothing more to teach me, that I was old beyond my years. "Trust an ex-fisherman to be handy with the hook," he said and drank my health with imported whiskey.

I had learned that the same network of commissions and escorting existed in most other Mexican resorts, but that there were places where foreign women lived and could be exploited more fully than places like Acapulco and Mazatlan, where they came and went on vacation packages. From what I could learn, the "fishing" would be best in the new resort of Puerto Vallarta, so I went there to see for myself. My only regret was that I hadn't gone sooner.

It's a much smaller town than Acapulco, of course. I might have been expected to miss the big city advantages, but I was a country boy, you'll remember, and found the smaller, more peaceful charms of Puerto Vallarta very much to my liking. My first night there, by the way, I spent with an American woman in her late forties, an episode that led to five days of rather pleasurable "employment" on the beach and dance floor and my acquisition of a Norelco electric shaver, a silk kimono, and my very first case of gonorrhea.

She was a strong and attractive woman and could have easily found less mercenary company in the bars, but she liked our arrangement, probably because she was in control. She was always on top in bed, or initiating sex in the shower or sea. She was the one who introduced me to the Ladies Bar at the Oro Verde Hotel. It's a funny thing, but when I walked into that lounge with her on my arm I instantly felt at home, as if I had known that room would be my "office", living room and performance stage for the next fifteen years. I took enough money out of that place to live on but I left my youth right there on that dance floor in the arms of women who had left their own youth somewhere else.

The Oro Verde was the central clearing-house for gigolos in Vallarta and it immediately felt very familiar and appropriate to me. It sits out from the main structure, with a commanding view of the sea and the sunset made so famous by "Night of the Iguana". I liked the large dance floor, the rosewood tables and captain chairs, the marimba bands for dancing, even their house sangria. In a short time I knew everyone there and was a member of that society. It was new life that suited me perfectly. I was no longer steering tourists into commissions; I became a hot spot myself, one of the tropical delights of Paradise. I was a tourist attraction.

Though it seemed natural at the time, as I look back on the Oro Verde I can see it was a somewhat peculiar scenario. I remember a friend comparing it to a livestock show or cock tournament. Every night around eight, or whatever time it would take to eat, shower and dress after leaving the beach for the day, the bar would start to fill up. The men would be mostly young and handsome, dressed casually flashy or in a white pants, Hawaiian mode. A few, like myself, were older and maintained our territory through class and mannerisms. Most of the men over twenty-five wore loose *guayabera* shirts like I did. There would always be a musician or two on the small stage, arranging equipment and chattering with the beach boys, but the music would not start until around ten. The musicians, I decided, were to advertise that there would be music later, and to keep things informal for drinking, conversing, and table-hopping in the meantime. The men would order their own drinks or wait for the invitations of the women.

The women were almost of a type; in their fifties and sixties, dressed in local *típica* clothes and expensive jewelry, deeply tanned. Some would wear Hawaiian muumuus, especially the fatter ones. There are a lot of Americans who have a

Hawaii fetish. If they are at a beach with palm trees, they want to see those Hawaiian idols and decorations. Mexico is a sort of cut-rate Hawaii for them. I mentioned that idea to one of my colleagues and he agreed, then said that Mexican gigolos are cut-rate Italians.

The women were, in some way, strong. Or I should say, powerful. They were *gringas* independent of men, "well-married, well-divorced or well-widowed" one of them once said. They were very much at home in Mexico and very accustomed to control and command. Many were long-term residents, like the famous circle that congregated at "La Palapa". Painters, sailors, alcoholics, adventuresses. Others were only seasonal residents, others short-term visitors that seemed to know about the Oro Verde and be very accustomed to the type of activity featured there.

Because my friend was right: it was a best-of-breed show. It was like a marketplace for gigolo customers to come shop around, and where we could lay out our wares. The women held auditions for companions, tried to tempt away consorts from other women and showed off their latest finds to their friends. Friends who would never say anything about the difference in age and general attractiveness.

Because that was the one most important thing about the Oro Verde: bought company was the accepted norm and nobody needed to be embarrassed about it. A woman once told me, "It's like a sexual opium den. Everybody is in the same boat and there's no room for pretense or false pride." An older woman dreamily dancing with her hands on the slender hips of a young stud who fetched her drinks and lit her cigarettes was accepted, normal behavior in the Oro Verde. One of my women called it a "gigolo ghetto"; it was, and perhaps still is, a sort of libido preserve. Anywhere else there would be those little looks that women dread.

For that matter, I think the young guys dreaded them, too. I had no sensitivity to looks or remarks, myself. I was what I was and used to it. When I was at the Oro Verde I was "at the shop". I wish I was sitting there now, looking out the big windows at Playa de los Muertos, listening to tropical dance music, sipping a fruity sangria and eyeing the dozens of couples in new clothes sliding around on that shiny hardwood floor.

My life in Vallarta was sweet and successful from the day I arrived. It's a pretty little whore of a town, with a slightly corrupt whiff of tropical mystique. Unlike Mazatlan or Acapulco, Vallarta is an Elizabeth Taylor kind of place, a place people go to look for a certain kind of experience. The kind of experience I was learning how to become. Sitting on the beach under the *palapas* sipping rum from a coconut and listening to jumpy music on "Radio Paradise", I could look up at wealthy homes, flashy colored flowers and birds, slim beautiful natives. A paradise where even money was as available as the ripe mangos on the trees. I applied myself to learning how to harvest that particular fruit.

This matter of money is, obviously, a quite delicate part of such a business. Most women have a need to nurture the illusion that there is romance, that they are giving gifts rather than merely paying for services rendered. And cash is the least romantic of gifts. On the other hand, a man needs only so much of clothes, jewelry, and sexy curios—what is requried is rent, your own car, your own retirement fund. The real difference between a professional like myself and the muscular beach boys that last only a few seasons is the ability to extract liquid assets. The odd thing is, the women don't really object to this, are only too glad to part with their money—the problem is inventing a scenario that will allow their social upbringing and feminine ego to do what they want to do in the first place. But now that I mention it, isn't that always the problem with a woman? And those who solve the problem find that the same techniques work equally well with all women.

First I began to realize that clothes, especially the resort and nightclub wear they most like to give you, are pathetically worthless for resale. A four-hundred-dollar tuxedo or "smoking" might be worth twenty on the resale market. Of course, fine clothes and appointments have their uses, image being so vital in this line of endeavor, but there are limits. I quickly figured out that my tastes would be refined and only include clothing from certain posh stores. . . stores that would allow me liberal exchange policies in exchange for kickbacks. I was inventing my craft as I learned it.

My first important inspiration came when I was taking pictures of myself with a woman, an extremely distressed heiress from San Francisco who spent her winters in Mexico overexposing herself to the sun, alcohol, pills, and men. She was a bit of a mess and at the time I didn't have enough English to understand her confidences. But she was a model of mental health and serenity as long as I was mounting her or as long as we were together in bed or naked and touching. I could think of myself as a sort of therapy, I suppose. Certainly less dangerous than the pills. Though ideally somewhat more expensive.

At any rate, I was arranging for some little beach urchin to take pictures of the two of us sharing a drink from a coconut (at the old Daiquiri Dick's on Playa De Los Muertos, I believe) when it hit me. I became quite enthusiastic about taking her picture, for my own souvenirs as well as for artistic "studies". My only regret was that I had to do it with her simple pocket snapshot camera. If only I still had my old Nikon, with its portrait lens that could have really done her justice. The next time she came south, she gave me a good quality 35mm camera with three lenses—worth over two hundred at the time, far more than my total worth or my expenses for five months.

Women love pictures. Even though many are very camera shy and have to be shot candidly or with much persuasion, another mildly annoying example of women having to be tricked or badgered into being given what they want. They keep the shots as trophies, or perhaps as amulets. They are always moved when I ask to keep their pictures for myself. I used to keep them in an old bronze frame from Tlaquepaque, frequently alleged to have once belonged to my sainted mother, which was hinged for easy changing of the current display.

My biggest problem was producing worthy shots. My friend Francisco, who ran the processing shop, helped by "ruining by overdevelopment" my first two rolls, laboriously producing some hazy impressionistic ("romantic", need I say) prints from the next, and meanwhile giving me a crash course in taking pictures that looked decent. I was astounded that there was actually some skill and forethought involved in such a simple and automatic thing as photography. I have gotten quite good over the years, by the way, especially at portraits. I could probably make a living just by taking pictures. Of women, at least.

When I sold the camera and felt the cash in my hand, more than I'd ever had at one time in my life, I knew I was on to something very good and big. Looking back on it, it was as though I had invented an industry. I'd never have cleared as much "teaching dancing". The camera charade became a standby, a hedge I never mentioned to my fellow *gringa* handlers. One of them would have bragged about it to belittle some woman who was quitting him and word would have gotten around very quickly. The women who admire us are a tight little clique really, bound by common interests. Like horse lovers or cat fanciers.

In addition to my first real "cash crop", the camera was my first practical lesson in value and liquidity. I started developing an eye for things that retained value, that could be quickly sold. I found out which cameras were more prized, which watches could be most easily disposed of. I was quite shocked to find out that there were watches priced in the thousands of dollars. The first time I recognized a Rolex on a man's wrist I couldn't take my eyes off it. It would have paid for a fine house in Acapulco, the price of the entire town of my birth. I was fascinated that such a little thing could be worth so much, so easily moved from one hand to the next.

Not that I was tempted to steal. I had long since gotten a true vocation, as the priests say; I had seen what could be done with women and that I had a talent in that direction which practically obligated me to develop it. Years later I laughed to remember staring at that watch: I was lying staring between the sprawled legs of a sleeping woman and I thought, "Such a small thing, yet so costly, yet so easily acquired and manipulated." Fortunately she didn't wake up. If she had met my eyes I don't think I could have stopped laughing.

I moved a long way off from cameras, didn't I? This is the way to talk, a lazy afternoon above the sea, good food and drinks at hand, your tape recorder handling all the details and organization so I can slip effortlessly through my memories. Are you aware that your own profession is fairly therapeutic? Between you with your microphone and this young man with his tray and cigarette lighter, we will do well here, become better adjusted to our lives.

So. Once I had a portfolio of presentable pictures (including some thrown in by my friend in the lab) I was established as both artist and collector and the women died to be photographed. To be included. . . do you see that? To be suitably commemorated. I can't overemphasize the importance of those pictures. . . or really comprehend it completely. They seemed to be challenged, or possibly threatened, by the faces from my past. The images brought up the whole issue of my amours being something less than exclusive and enduring notably less than until the end of time. Yet they were evidence of something; maybe just that I actually remembered women, that whatever was happening was not just of the moment. They gave a certain validity, the kind of secret, subtle permanence women so desire. I think they compared themselves to those other women—who I always referred to as "friends" or "models"—and, I think, found them easier competition than their own imaginations. Whatever it might be that women are always competing for.

But, naturally, I was always tragically without a decent camera and thus frequently received them as thoughtful gifts. I always accepted them gratefully and as if I was as much surprised as delighted. Since there was nowhere in Vallarta to buy a quality camera, the women always ended up inquiring of my friend Cisco at the processing shop, or at their hotel desk, with the same result, and ended up buying one in almost new condition from a German wildlife photographer who just happened to be staying in the Hotel Oceano and selling off some of his gear before going back to Munich. It was a fairly nice Minolta and I took pains to keep it in good condition through the dozens of times it was given to me.

The German (actually an American army deserter from Wisconsin who enjoyed doing Teutonic accents) was getting about twenty-five dollars every time it changed hands, a little surcharge I paid for having to do things that way so they'd think it was all their own idea. I had to pay for being "surprised". I put away around three thousand dollars thanks to that camera, and gradually acquired a nice leather bag, lenses, and accessories—all gifts from admirers, of course.

The savings were important to me, though day to day living expenses were meaningless. I always lived and ate at some woman's expense, usually at the best hotels and restaurants. I've stayed in the Bougambillias penthouse, the Garza Blanca's cabaña at four hundred dollars a night, in the "presidential" suite at the Oro Verde. Not my favorite hotel for sleeping; too much like living over the shop.

I expanded the camera ploy to guitars. Like most Mexican Don Juans, I play passably and know ways to appear more proficient than I am. I even sing a bit, mostly relying on the impact of the melancholia, drama and romance of old

Mexican songs. Later I worked it with diving equipment, though that was trickier since there are places to rent it. An expedition to some remote cove like Los Ayala or Nadaderos for nude diving and beachcombing usually did the trick. The advent of the Walkman was wonderful—one of the most liquid medium-ticket items ever made. The perfect gift for a music lover like myself (so frequently an *aficionado* of exactly the same type music as the giver) and instantly disposable, often for more than what it had cost new.

I developed a predilection for gold coin jewelry and was wise enough not to resell it, but to save the coins themselves. I sold most of them when gold went to six hundred dollars an ounce in the mid-seventies. Coins are a good investment in Mexico where there are volume money-changing houses everywhere. I found that one can seed "hints"; that wearing a gold peso pieces can generate similar gifts. I cultivated a collection of clothes and accessories with seahorse motifs for a time, which led to gifts of others in precious metals—a common item in Vallarta. Sometimes I would reinforce that impulse by creating fond associations with the large bronze seahorse that used to stand on Playa de Los Muertos. I became a master of the blessed gift of receiving. My dream "gift" was an automobile, one goal I never achieved. Sad, but there are great soccer players who never won the World Cup, no?

An even more delicate question than money is the matter of romance itself, and it is the major problem that any gigolo with staying power must be able to solve, if not actually understand. There is no problem for a muscle boy to attach himself to a woman for a quick stand, especially in a situation where she will not be seen with him. There are very few women who will flourish their young studs in public. The prominent Vallarta painter Martha Gilbert is a flagrant exception, something I always admired in her.

But, as I say, our young stallion isn't going to take anything away with him—just kickbacks, maybe some macho undershorts. He's too young or too egotistical to understand how to play the long game. Perhaps if he were capable of moving somewhat beyond the business of "my penis is such a hot commodity, doesn't it just destroy you?" If he were to seem vulnerable, cry a little one night, appeal to her motherly instincts, make her feel like he needed an older, wiser mentor to shine him up, educate him, get him good clothes and attitudes, he might have something on the line. Women love to play Pygmalion—a fact to which I owe much of my own education. An education more valuable for having been channeled into areas pleasing to older, richer women.

I find it interesting that women are always most intrigued by the way I handled the financial side of things (as you have been in this interview) while men always lead around to the physical nature of it. Since I assume you have some men in your readership, let me touch on a few things men seem curious about.

In the first place, I am not some sort of sexual super-athlete. I assume I am fairly normal in that regard. Though I will say that total emotional detachment grants a certain advantage, which is to say power. Of the many jokes so intrinsic to sex (either God or the Devil has a formidable sense of humor) the most ironic is that a man's staying power is. . . what is the phrase?. . . "reversely proportionate" to his emotional involvement. The love-drunk Romeo faints into climax at a touch while the cold pimp perseveres through brutal and devastating sex-lashings. As I said; a joke on us all. But women are generally looking for certain companionship or presentation qualities, not marathon sex. Thank God.

I can't say too much, in that respect, about the advantages of oral sex. It was not something I picked up right away. American women seem to expect this attention—I guess it is more common in that country. Most Mexican men find it objectionable and degrading. We are by no means an avant-garde nation sexually. I myself have developed a taste for it, even though at one time I could only do it by closing my eyes and thinking of more pleasant activities.

Oral skill is a vital weapon (or should I say tool?) for a sexual professional, as you will understand; so I pushed myself to develop the ability and to overcome my initial revulsion at what is, and let's admit it, an extremely unnatural thing to do. There is no point in a man of my experience being less than frank about the fact that satisfying a woman is a demanding exertion, particularly the somewhat neurotic types my clients tend to be, and especially to the point of breaking them down into absolute docility. If I can bring them to orgasms before I even begin to ply my true manhood then I am well ahead of the game.

Sometimes I could even accommodate an "employer" to her fullest satisfaction and have some energy left over for my own pleasures later, so it was certainly worth it to prepare the field, you might say. Of course, oral intercourse requires neither physical exertion nor any degree of arousal. I'm not sure if it was really a French innovation; but if they hadn't invented it, I would have had to do so myself.

But my business was mainly one of attitude and posture. Is it not so often true when dealing with women? We develop poses to complement theirs. Very few women, almost none, will employ the straightforward "here is the money, where is the sex?" approach that men will accept. And they know better than to buy the idea that some handsome, winsome, muscular young stud is in romantic love with a chubby, fifty year-old divorcee. You have to play it just right. What worked best for me, once I got the experience and—how can I put this?—"spiritual weight" to put it across, was a sort of bittersweet irony. Like, "We're people of the world and we know what we're doing, but even in that there is something of respect and affection."

I would be like a stylized actor getting away with extravagant, flowery sentimentality by keeping an ironic edge behind it. . . and behind that just a gleam of the idea that there might be some sort of real true love hiding behind that charming defensive crust. None of this was a question of their believing anything stated, but of being offered an attitude acceptable to their self-respect.

Perhaps the French did not invent cunnilingus, but they definitely have a gift for the ironic, worldly-wise mode and American women have a distinct weakness for it. I would call a study of French cinema invaluable to any gigolo past his mid-twenties. I've seen every such film I could and don't need to understand the dialogue to absorb the moves and attitudes. I was also indebted from an early age to the American films of Humphrey Bogart though, again, I didn't always know exactly what was being said. In fact. I have reduced women to soft clay in my hands by "forgetting" my English in an "emotional" moment and flooding them with Spanish sounds accompanied by visuals ala Bogart and Belmondo.

It's a subtle game and I'm sure you understand I don't do it consciously. It works best with the relatively intelligent, educated woman—which is the kind I prefer anyway, since I essentially live with them for the duration of our affairs. I don't really care what they look like. Obviously. Though I sometimes pay attention to what their daughters look like. If I had to summarize my own tastes in women for most of my mature life, I'd have to say, "Somebody's twenty-year-old daughter." Their attitudes towards me are usually quite complex and by no means totally positive. They often resent my attentions to their mother and treat me contemptuously, which can make things quite delicious when their curiosity and sense of competition gets the upper hand. As Enrique told me at the very start, it's not a bad life and the *mondonga* is just gravy. My life in "Paradise" was good, rich and sweet. But I decided things could be a little better and ended up losing everything.

My decision to move to Tijuana was an unfortunate one, a disaster really, although it seemed a good idea when it was suggested by one of my colleagues. He remarked my touch with American women and said that I should go up to the border where I would be surrounded by them. I thought about that, and Tijuana's growing reputation as an economic boomtown. I was no longer young and no longer made much of a beach boy.

My growing sophistication suggested larger cities but in most Mexican cities my English skills and North American urbanity would have presented me little advantage. In fact even my "sophistication" was worldly, international and American; most Mexican women would have considered me an effete, abstract poseur. I had several thousand dollars saved and thought of using it as a seed to make more, the way a fisherman slices his first fish into bait for more fish. At the border, in a land of automobiles, chromium and green dollars, I could certainly do better. Maybe I could even marry a rich woman and secure my future, while I still had some vitality and promise. So I made the move to the north, the one worst move of my life.

Like many Mexicans, I considered Tijuana a world apart from Mexico itself, a strange mutant city far north of a wasteland. I got on the bus in much the same spirit that a man would step on a shuttle to the moon. I was hopeful, but very apprehensive. The trip was boring and painful. But somewhere in Sonora something happened that I will never forget. I had a brief taste of a fairly ordinary young woman, an encounter that stands in my memory like a lighthouse above the sea of so many other women. It may have been the most wonderful sex of my life, it may have been the worst. But it was definitively the most memorable.

She got on with her family in Mochis or Guaymas but had to sit in the back away from them since the bus was very crowded. She was in her early twenties and looked like the typical downcast Mexican daughter, but with a little more knowing glance and unselfconscious movement. Perhaps she had been married and come back to the family roost. When the opportunity presented, I moved over to sit beside her.

We started with small talk that never pretended to be anything but flirtation. I felt that she had marked me when she first came down the aisle. I slumped in my seat and spoke to her without turning my head, since her parents occasionally looked around to check up on her. She maintained a practiced primness, but I could feel the increasing heat of her thigh by mine, sense the direction of her interest. Thank God for the never-ending desert night; in a few hours we were alone in the crowded bus, everyone else either asleep or in that strange trance that highway buses create. I draped a blanket over us and began to explore her under its cover.

She was not coy at all, and seemed as interested an explorer as I was. We began a long, strange foreplay, a rising and falling excitement that went on for hours and miles. Many times I was at a peak of passion, would have thrown her down and ravaged her like a bloodshot bull. . . but we could do nothing to attract attention. Her peasant father slept just three rows in front of us, and without any doubt had a cane knife in his waistband. We found each other in small sections and pieces, experienced our releases in installments. At one point we were both squeezing the vital points of the other, our hands wet and clenched, though our breathing was controlled and our postures erect and rigid. But I was staring right into her eyes. Without saying a word, I felt something pass between us that I never understood, a greater communication than all the worthless words I have wasted on all the women in the world.

I can't explain why I say this, but in the dark of that bus seat I lived a normal life for a few hours, just a man sharing pleasure with a willing woman. It was almost like I was a normal lover struggling for leverage and advantage with a normal woman. For a very short time in my life, money was meaningless, experience beside the point. She would never know she was in the hands of an expert. Not that it makes any difference.

It seems to be a secret that sex is not a good arena for competition, or even competence. I felt something that might have been love, or it might have been sadness. Or maybe a realization of what I was coming to, one of those sudden moments that start ambushing us when we get more than forty years. . . awareness of spent youth and paths it is too late to travel.

We grappled in the darkness as the desert rolled by the windows, intent on grasping our pleasure from the technical problems of the situation. We were unable to lie down and had to keep our heads in sight in case her parents turned around to look at her. Fortunately they slept as we squirmed and squirted. Occasionally somebody would walk past to the bathroom in the rear and catch us in some obvious moment. I remember at one point that she had turned to face me and I was hammering my hand into her. My arm was under a blanket, but the blanket was jumping with the motion when a short Indian walked by and gave us a flat stare. On his way back up the aisle, we were resting with our eyes closed, though my hand was still inside her, my wrist lay lightly on her thigh. He touched my shoulder just a moment and I jumped. He looked right in my eyes and smiled, pulling his lower eyelid down to mean he'd seen a secret.

Later we found that if I slid sideways into her seat she could lift her skirt and sit on me, giving us a penetration that was frustrating not only for it's limited depth but because we could not move except very slowly. But I manipulated her with my hands and when I felt her climax in shown by her hard breathing and inner clutching, something forgotten and unexpected broke loose inside me and I filled her with my seed. I will never forget that when we got to the station and she went off with her family without daring a backward look, I glanced back at the seat and saw a shiny smear where she had drained on the dirty fabric. It caused me a sudden *tristesa*, a feeling in my entrails of things long lost.

I have remembered her often over the years, dreamed of having pursued her off the bus and claimed her, taking her off to. . . To what? What did I have that was worth as much as the simple beastly act any couple does every night without thinking anything of it? It is probably hindsight to say so, but I think that bus trip and the touch of that girl was the start of my decline. I was almost aware of it as I stepped down into the bus station. When I walked out into the *centro* of Tijuana, I was almost aware that I had made the biggest mistake of my life.

For one thing, the city itself was as ugly and dirty as it is now, the climate as bad. Women, it turned out, are not as susceptible to my talents when at home, and most of those going to Tijuana were only shopping, not staying nor seeking affairs. Since I had avoided military conscription as a young man (and what young man in my position would have gone off to sleep in a barracks full of men instead of the beds of tourist women?) I could not get a passport to cross into the United States. What little opportunity existed was short-term and of low financial quality. And there was a great deal of very experienced competition. In Tijuana sex is sold straight with no embellishments or pretty wrappings. "No chaser" as the *gabachos* say. I realized how much of my former success was created by a vacation mentality, the allure of the beach and the special romantic magic or both Acapulco and Vallarta.

Tijuana had other disadvantages. The cold troubled me a great deal and my first few winters I had severe grippe and influenza much of the time. The locals complain that immigrants from the South bring in diseases and it's true. As one of those immigrants I suppose I shouldn't complain, but my impression of the town was that of a pit of malevolent microbes. The cold affected me in a more subtle way, as well. I retracted and restricted from the cold, became slow and sluggish like a frozen iguana. I started to become an indoors sort of person, losing the healthy outdoor look I'd always had. I had little appetite or sex drive during the winter months, became silent and sullen.

Naturally, this affected my work. I was becoming less attractive, less. . . involved. I was going through my savings very fast. As my health, appearance, and finances sunk lower, I also started to lose the most vital asset of any man who needs success with women—my self-confidence. That indefinable aspect of male presentation accounts for more than just the way we talk, walk, and carry ourselves (though all are more important in the conquest of women than things like money and looks). There is also. . . and I am quite positive of this, though there is no way for scientists to prove it. . . some subtle emanation women receive and react to without knowing it. Perhaps there is an odor, like fear or musk. A satisfied, self-confident man has something women want. They see married men as more attractive than bachelors, men who have recently had sex as more attractive than those who have been without it for a long time, like prisoners or sailors. On the other hand sexual deprivation, and more especially desperation, is like wearing an invisible halo that warms women away. This is something men in my profession learn as they age, though few would put it in words.

It may even be a principle that applies universally, not just to sex. While I have had almost no business with banks or lenders, I'm told that they like to give money to people who have money, but are reluctant to share it with the poor. Again, a matter of confidence. For both parties, now that I think of it. One of my clients, an attractive financial executive in her late fifties, once told me that confidence is the secret coin of all money dealings, that nobody would even accept cash or gold if they didn't have confidence that they could exchange it for something else in the future. Similarly, bad times come when people feel bad, good times when people feel good and confident in themselves and their prospects. The economy, she said (and I have no reason or qualifications to doubt her) is little more than a massive confidence game. She also told me a line from a North American Negro song that applies to what I've been talking about, "Those that have shall get, those that don't shall lose." I was certainly finding it to be the case.

Sorry to have slipped off into abstracts; perhaps it's just to avoid discussing that very unhappy and terrifying period of my life. When I say "terrifying", I'm not exaggerating. I was living day to day, squeezing out a very fragile income in the lobby bars of Caesar's and the Nelson, perhaps picking up someone to "guide" at the bullring on Sundays or recommending myself as a betting counselor at the Jai Alai (where I often presented myself as an ex-player and sometime coach/manager). The future of my trade appeared darker every day. My clothes were getting worn and used-looking, my health and looks suffering, my attitude hardening into an unattractive mask. There was little, I realized, to separate me from the growing tide of ignorant, poverty-struck *"Juan Nadies"* coming into Tijuana and trying ridiculous schemes to part gringos from their dollars. A foreign woman would be offered sexual opportunities on every corner she passed, and would become used to brushing off the advances of pushy salesmen in front of every junky little store. What did I have to offer, really? What would keep me from a career of washing windshields or urging young soldiers into the foul sex bars that used to line Avenida Revolución?

Among my personal disadvantages in Tijuana was a lack of the net of friends, colleagues, and co-operators I had built in the South without thinking much about it. Nobody in Baja California owed me any favors, nobody paid for any services, nobody referred me to any clients, nor them to me. I had thought I would quickly establish connections in the new area as I had in Vallarta, but I never did. I was older, of course, and the real allies in our lives are made when we are young. Also Tijuana had (and still has) a more closed attitude, an infection, I suppose, from the famous "cold and calculating" temperament north of the border. I was merely a new competitor, one of thousands arriving every week.

There was no focal point for my talents, no Oro Verde, no beach, no "Golden Zone", no hotels frequented by foreign tourists. The situation was impossible but, I'm sorry to admit, I stayed there out of ego and stupidity until I was trapped, my hard-won savings spent, unable to afford even to leave. I was losing the game I had always won, the game I'd partially invented and made my own mark on, and I was getting addicted to losing. If that sounds strange, notice compulsive gamblers in their activities. They can quit when winning, but when they lose they can't pull themselves away, will borrow or steal to keep playing. Men losing at love are the same way and women even more so: milking each defeat, more committed when being abandoned than when in control. I was no different myself, it turns out.

It was nothing but possibilities that tempted and trapped me; possibilities that refused to become realities. I could see the incredible, careless *Yanqui* wealth at close range, watch the hypnotic Northern television with its casual treatment of idle sexuality and feverish commercial announcements of vulnerability to spending money on almost anything. I saw *gringas* at their loosest and most sluttish, another full color announcement of indiscriminate availability and screaming needs neither recognized nor understood. It all seemed so ready, so easy. I broke myself trying to get a hook into it.

Not that there was a complete lack of women coming to Tijuana those days, and not that they weren't interested in some "World Level" experience. But they were more interested in "colorful" and "*folklórico*" Mexican men: bullfighters, mariachis. These things are taken in perspective in the South but at the border, "Mexican" experiences, however ungenuine or out-of-place, are in greater demand. I became an ex-matador many times, complete with some ears, tails, *banderillas* and other souvenirs. But it was a disguise that worked only in private, with women I had isolated from the herd. I could never be introduced to anyone as a matador, nor be able to go to the *corrida* with anyone who believed me to be a *torero*. This, despite the fact that there were several fake matadors at the time, impressing *gringas* at the ranchos and hailed as such by accomplices in restaurants like Taurino and El Tablón. I myself was living on a very thin diet and it was starting to wear me down.

Worse, I was starting to think of myself as inferior, as cheap. Though I been too proud to ever think of myself as a whore, I started to see myself as morally dirty and compromised. I made bitter jokes over too many drinks in the Zona Roja, an area I increasingly frequented. I think I went there to look down on the prostitutes, to make myself feel like I was better than they were. If that was my intention, I failed. Notice the curious idea that as I lost respect for myself for failing to provide sex for money, I was starting to lose self-respect for providing it in the first place. The mind is disposed to draw wild conclusions. . . then leave us to suffer with them.

One afternoon, in a canyon up behind San Antonio de los Buenos, I saw a very thin old coyote nosing around some dry holes in the ground and had an extremely unsettling thought. What happens when a coyote or wolf or shark gets too weak from hunger to be able to kill another meal? Many times the cold weather here at the border has chilled me to my bones, but that was the coldest I've ever felt in my life.

I'll tell you the truth, even though you might not believe it: I went directly from there to a church. I didn't really understand why. Was I going to pray for God to help me in finding women with whom to fornicate for money? I was never more aware of myself as a whore, and for the very first time I called myself that name in my mind. But I went into the church anyway, a small neighborhood chapel in San Antonio, and immediately felt calmer and less frightened, even though I had never been religious, had not been in a church since childhood.

47

I sat and stared at their peeling painting of the Virgin of Guadalupe, serene and pure in her cloak of sacred blue sky. I walked up and looked closely at her facial expression, knelt to examine her. This is the way God manifests to us Mexicans; as a pale-skinned woman whose virginity survives even childbirth, whose purity survives even the drip of blood from her wounded heart, who brings the sky down to the soiled and impure earth.

I felt no dramatic urgings, no hot tears or pangs; but when I walked out of that church I had a feeling that the Virgin did not despise me, that God would not condemn me for being what I was, what he had made me to be. Looking back on that experience, I have no impulse to change or be "saved"; but I got respect for an institution I had once ridiculed. . . the confession. Now I firmly believe that confession is good for the soul and brings forgiveness. Even now, so aware of the nearness of the end of my life, I find forgiveness in me whenever I squarely face who I am and what I have done. If I end up in hell, I'm sure there are tormented women there who will need more than ever a taste of whatever it is they find in me.

Well. I'm not used to discussing matters like that with others. In fact, I have never mentioned that moment in the church to anyone else before. More of your therapy of microphone and printing press, I suppose. The modern confessional. You hadn't thought that the life of a man paid for his sex would have such theological implications, did you? Neither did I. But before I leave what is really an uncomfortable subject for me, I have to mention that three days after my audience with the coyote, Virgin and Holy Spirit, a friend took me, for the first time, to Rosarito Beach and my life turned around as if by magic. I don't put too great a credence in such matters, but a man would be a fool to deny them. It seems possible to me that respect is more important than belief.

My friend, who I had known in Vallarta, was working in the Rosarito Beach Hotel. As soon as we walked through the lobby doors, I knew there was something there, a special quality. . . you could call it "tropical romance". I looked at the murals of Southern jungles with beautiful women holding birds and handsome men with machetes and fishing nets. I saw the Aztec artwork. I looked at the tile pool with its fountain and lounge chairs, saw the tables and bar out on the beach. It looked wonderful to me, like a memory come back to life. I had a definite feeling, like my first time in the Oro Verde. And in fact the Hotel became another "office" for me; but maybe because of the changes I had experienced in Tijuana I saw myself instead as a fixture of the Hotel. I learned that the town was a vacation community and started patrolling the beach and hotels, liking everything I saw.

Mainly what I saw was my principal stock of trade, neurotic American divorcees desperate for reassurance, rebuilt esteem, and the quick oblivion of satiated flesh. And quite willing and able to pay the price of that desperation. If anything, I found such women in Rosarito to be even more insecure than my former clients in the South. The Rosarito *gringas*, whether divorced or still married, had also run away to Mexico, but had not dared go so far, were still holding onto their world at an arm's length, many going back and forth to gather new insults, disillusions, and damages to be repaired. I took a room in a house not far from the hotel and quickly found myself very much at home.

Though my basic approach was unchanged, in Rosarito I moved into a different focus and rhythm than what I'd been used to before. I started becoming less a vacation indulgence and more a sort of "boyfriend". This was partly because many of the women I came to know were more-or-less permanent residents with their own homes but also because there was now less difference, if any, between my age and that of my clients. It was acceptable for them to be seen with me, for me to meet their friends and children. And especially, I noticed, their ex-husbands. I always rose to those occasions, completely the cultivated and mysterious man of the world, but personable and with a common touch. Much better than he thought she would do or, there was the hint, had done in the past.

This sort of thing helped re-mold me into a sort of mature period (I was quite taken at the time by the films of David Niven) and to restore my damaged self-confidence. Perhaps it's the same thing they are now calling self-esteem. I even read one of the many *auto-estima* books available in Spanish, though I was unimpressed by its recommendations. But even though my character had been restored and nurtured by the feverish, addictive needs of wealthy, educated women (as well as the envy of their friends and ex-spouses) I had some permanent damage during my years of scrambling and terror in Tijuana. My health never fully recovered and still troubles me. The lungs, the liver, the prostate. . . the usual. Though I heard it said that the slightly gaunt look became me very well. Made me look like I'd suffered, I recall hearing. Another used the word "poetic". She probably had it confused with "tubercular" due to all the operas and novels about poets living in hovels and dying of consumption. When you have recovered your belief in yourself, it seems, even disease and poverty become fashionable.

So I became a boyfriend, living in nicely-appointed beach homes with hot water, king-sized waterbeds, giant televisions with parabolic antennas, maid service. I have even been given the run of a house at times, staying there while the owner was off in Los Angeles or Phoenix doing whatever she did with her "real" life. The idea of leaving me alone in a house seemed so incredibly stupid that I was never even tempted to take advantage of it by selling everything off. My "girlfriends" knew that my affections were changeable and only temporary, so I did not have to deal with jealousies or worry about gossip. Everyone knew what I was, and nobody made any move to hide it, so nobody had to name it.

When a live-in girlfriend was out of town, I immediately "played the field". This was certainly not due to great carnal appetites on my part, but good business. For one thing, even with a roof over my head, I had to eat. So I earned my daily bread by the sweat, if not of my forehead, at least of my body. I often silently lamented all the drinks and meals that were bought for me in Rosarito without bringing me a single commission. The places would have paid me for new business, but not for "landing" women who were already regular customers.

Besides, I found it good business to move around a little, not to let any one contract get too stable or stale. I had seen friends become full-time "boyfriends" and hadn't liked what I saw. A pet dog existence in the hands of a clinging or demanding woman; no control nor, ultimately, security. When they are too sure of you, they get tired of you. Otherwise they would have stayed with their husbands. I tried to keep my subtle "mysterious" quality a proven factor.

My life and "loves" were well-known, but not greatly remarked in the rather small permanent American community. I was popular in expatriate bars like El Nido and Rene's where the local gringos gathered, and was seen by the men as a companionable source of local language and legend and by the women as a high-ticket but affordable sex appliance. One woman with a huge house on the cliffs by the Quinta Mar did much to further my education in art and English literature. Incredibly, I first read "Don Quixote" in English. I think of education as something contagious, contactable from one person to another like disease. I have become a well-educated man largely through a sort of osmosis. When she mentioned a poem called "Paradise Regained" the phrase made a deep impression on me. I remember sitting in the luxury of her living room, looking out at the sea, with that phrase running around in my mind. Somehow I had left Paradise, somehow I had found it again. I don't understand any of it but feel very grateful. It was a very full period of my life and I still guard a deep affection for Rosarito, even what it has become in recent years.

Some of the local bartenders and beach types started calling me "El Pelicano". The way they pronounced it was a pun on pelican, but means a man with gray hair. Once again, I was a fishing bird. I mentioned that to a friend, an owner of rental horses who sometimes led his string by the Hotel patio to let me know that one of the women on board might be worth meeting. He laughed and said that next I would be called "Gaviota". It's another pun; meaning a seagull, but also a crude term used in the south to refer to a prostitute too old to do any business. Maybe it would be a good nickname to put on my gravestone.

I didn't get rich here in the North, but I didn't have to clean windshields, either. Rosarito was better than I deserved and I was happy enough to live in modest but gentle circumstances for my remaining useful years. More years than I care to count up, I can tell you. Please forgive me if I've been a little vague on numbers and dates. Not only is my memory losing interest in such matters, I don't want to really fix my presence too closely in anybody's mind. There are women who might read this and think thoughts. There are doubtless, for that matter, jealous husbands.

I can fix time in one way, though; I have a daughter of thirteen years who I sired here in Rosarito. Her name is Xochil and her mother was the daughter of one of my first clients at the Hotel. She was an equestrienne, riding with the *escarmuza*, the Mexican "cowgirls" who compete in tournaments of pretty horsemanship. She was a fiery and egotistical girl, but beautiful. . . and she could ride like a cloud, like a dream.

I used to borrow her pony, telling her I was riding, but actually using the animal to pose as an injured ex-polo player to impress some rather silly women that spent a few weeks each year at the Hotel. When she discovered this she confronted me angrily in the stables, striking me with her whip.

It was a display that led to me peeling her tight riding breeches off and watching her gallop violently astride me in the hay. I was surprised by her decision to have the baby (the only child I ever fathered, to the best of my knowledge), and even more by the fact that she never told anyone I was the father. Except the girl, of course, when she was old enough to know.

I'm still "older than my years", as I was as a boy, but it's much less an advantage now. I'm sure you'd take me for much older than sixty-four and my body seems to be accelerating its collapse. If my lungs don't hurry up and kill what's left of me, this prostate situation will beat them to it. I've entirely lost my manhood and, unlike trumpeters who lose their lip or boxers who lose their legs, I have no real way to compensate, no technique to atone for the failure of mere meat.

It's embarrassing to realize that my personal style, my personality in fact, has been molded around what American women like and find amusing. I have become a caricature to a certain extent—a pet Ricardo Montalban, a Latino David Niven. I became a type, I suppose: a certain model of a certain commodity of a certain known value. Yet I determined that price myself. And women paid that price gladly, even though the very knowledge that they are paying at all is the highest price most women could ever pay.

I find one thing ironic and extremely amusing these days; the woman I spend the most time with, a sort of lover, friend companion, and (I lament to say it) a bit of a caretaker. She's younger than I am (who isn't any more?), maybe around fifty. She has a wonderful heart, very unsophisticated and genuine. She has no money at all—I met her through one of her small-time smuggling schemes. She's also very fat, and very plain. She'd fit right in at the Oro Verde in a tropical muumuu and twenty pounds of rattling jewelry. I'm sure I don't have to explain why I find my relationship with her so amusing. She also hires my daughter Xochil to work part-time in her little travel agency. That's funny, too.

My daughter by the way, is a very beautiful girl. Like her mother was. Her attitudes towards me are not complicated at all. She loves me, adores me. When she leans over and kisses me she's so beautiful it almost stops my heart; I can see that love shining out of her face like the sun and I can barely look at it. But I can! I can accept that undiluted adoration, look it right in the eye. That's another thing my life has brought me to. If I could sum up right now what it all meant. . . and I'm sure this will sound strange. . . it's that I have been loved. I have been desired and adored and enamored by women like few men have ever been. And even though I am a man of very little philosophy, I strongly feel that the universe does not run out of balance. . . and that somehow I have given as much as I have received out of balance. . . and that somehow I have given as much as I have received.

III. *CHILES BRAVO'S* WORLD TOUR

In a recent story in this publication, I mentioned *mestizaje*, the mixing of European and American elements which produced the Mexican people and the Mexican cuisine. It is unusual for such processes to be noted with dates and locations among the battles and assassinations of a civilization's "official" histories, but in the case of Mexico's *mestizaje culinario*, there are official records. In 1521 Hernan Cortes celebrated his conquest of the Aztec capital by throwing a grand feast for his captains and men; an event recorded by Bernal Diaz del Castillo, eyewitness historian of the Conquest. It has occurred to me that North Americans could view that banquet as a grotesque parody of the first Thanksgiving feast. Instead of hungry pilgrims humbly receiving gifts of turkey, corn and potatoes from friendly Indians, the feast of Tenochtitlan that gave birth to the national cuisine was a matter of triumphant soldiers commanding tribute at the point of a sword.

The Spaniards had brought their own ideas of eating. Diaz reported that there were pigs and wine at the table, but no wheat since the local cultivation of wheat had just been started from three grains a black slave accidentally found in a sack of rice. But what caught Diaz' interest was the presence at that table of corn, chocolate, chia, tomatoes, *chiles*, squash, papayas, guavas, jicama, vanilla, and turkey; in addition to

American produce such as *mamey, colorin, chayote, pitamonte, anona, chirimoya, zapote, chicozapote,* and *jacote* that haven't enjoyed foreign names or exploitation.

Experiments certainly resulted. A taco of corn tortilla, cheese, and chicken became possible for the first time. Turkey could be eaten with rice, pork seasoned with *chiles*. Wine could be mixed with tropical juices. The gestation of the Mexican diet continued along with the interpenetration of the races, often symbolized by Cortes taking into his arms the beautiful interpreter La Malinche, who had served his expedition much as the famous Northern Indian Sacajawea, and bore children to Cortes. While the taming of North America is generally portrayed as a struggle or task, that of the South always seems to carry sexual symbolism, to have the hint of rape about it. Our famous murals bristle with it, as full of suggestive Spanish pikes and lances as they are of evil priests, fat financiers, and noble suffering Indians—generally faceless and bare-breasted. This pregnant thread of folklore runs through Cortes' personal conquest of La Malinche, the interbreeding of Spanish and Indians, and even the seductions of culture and cooking.

La Malinche is often referred to as "La Chingada", meaning raped or taken. A university classmate used to tell us that there was a big difference between the English settlement of North America and the Spanish conquest of the South: in the North the Indians were killed, in the South they were enslaved and raped. Then she would always say, "And which is worse?" This was seen as wisdom in our circle at the time, but I never had any doubt that it would be better to be a raped slave than to be dead.

Perhaps it is my own lack of purity and character, but I don't believe that there is any fate worse than death. I prefer to consider that while life and fate remain there can be hope and faith. I once told my friend, "Even if I were raped and with child, the child would be mine." That idea was very poorly received. We were idealists then; which is to say, of a privileged class. But who will argue against motherhood? Half-breeds, bastards and *hijos de la chingada:* all are their mother's sons. This is a central fact of sex much deeper than the tawdry lingerie of glamour and sin we throw around it and I see it powerfully symbolized by a primordial element of the *cocina mexicana,* the *chile*—a plant that conquered the world that seized it up and carried it off.

When I speak of *chiles,* don't think that I am limiting myself to *jalapeños* and the red powder sold in supermarkets. There are at least two hundred different kinds, each with its certain flavor and color. They differ in the amount of "fire", not all are *picante.* The red, green, and yellow vegetables North Americans think of as "peppers" are really *chiles.* All *chiles,* from the tiny blistering *chile de arbol* to a cool green bell pepper are of the *capsicum* family—very distinct from the *piper nigrum* family that includes black peppercorns. How did such confusion enter the English language? It shouldn't surprise anyone that it can be traced to Christopher Columbus. The poor fellow was capable enough with ships, maps, and queens to find the new Eden; but he was no Adam when it came time to give out names. Though it is notable everyone uses the names he gave, even though everyone knows he was mistaken. We might even suspect of him of some marketing skills, since pepper was extremely valuable at the time, worth its weight in silver. If red "pepper" was as hot as the black kind, who would care if it was actually ground cayenne, a *chile* in the same family as the *arbol?*

Especially since the wild *chiles* originally discovered by Columbus were small red balls like holly berries which, when dried, would have looked something like red peppercorns. Those wild hot berries were *tepin chiles,* related to many small, bright red *chiles* eaten today like the pea-sized *pequin* (known to have been served by at Monteczuma's courts in *pipian* sauce), fiery sausage-shaped little *chile de arbol,* and the triangular *pico de gallo,* named after their resemblance to the beaks of cocks. The first *chiles* to be seen in Europe were very similar to the first *chiles* on Earth, which originated as vines in the Amazon jungles thousands of years ago. All the hundreds of colors and sizes and flavors of *chiles* are of the genus *capsicum*, which flowered out of crude rain forest vines. The bright red fruits were an obvious advantage to the proto-*chile* plants; they caught the eyes of birds, which enabled the *chiles* to spread their seed through the crude but effective methods of ingestion and excretion.

The evolutionry advantage of producing the unique and powerful chemical capasicin, which gives all *chiles* their "bite", was not obvious at first, but at least ten thousand years ago their unique chemical ingredient capasicin caught the palates of humans and the *chiles* were spread farther and developed more widely as their flavors were cherished. Carefully preserved *chiles* have been found in Peruvian tombs dating to five centuries before Christ, when the pharaohs were being sent to eternity with nothing to show for their lives but mere gold and slaves.

This reverence for the powers of capasicin caused a more deliberate spread of the *chile* plants, aided by their trade value, the ease in growing them (far easier than temperamental pepper plants), and the ease with which they cross-pollinate to create new kinds of *chile* with different tastes and degrees of spiciness; the same holy magic that has unfolded hundreds of powerful and distinctive plants from the seeds of those original hot berries. The random mixing (if random is what you'd call it) became purposeful as gardeners' hands molded the results to suit eye and palate. By the time the Europeans "discovered" the Aztecs, the *chile* had spread throughout the Americas. Once they were taken as an equivalent for pepper, the Europeans started spreading them much more efficiently than the birds had been able to.

Within one hundred years of the discovery of the Americas, the Spanish and Portuguese had carried the *chile* around the world. In Africa and Madagascar *chiles* became an integral part of the local diet. Asian dishes thought of as extremely traditional, like Korean *kim chee* or the hot foods of southern China and Thailand, date back only to the arrival of *chile* in the sixteenth century, as in Europe the paprika of Hungarian foods is powdered *pimento chile*. *Chiles* were cultivated in India and the East Indies, where the real "Indians" adopted their flavor and spiciness. Columbus had sent spices to the Indies, rather than bringing them back. Today over three quarters of the people in the world eat *chiles* as part of their normal diet; *chiles* are the most commonly used spice on earth. From the point of view of the *chile* plant, Europeans were merely more efficient birds, a mechanism by which it could extend its empire.

The process by which the world became as dependent on *chile* as it is on other famous American addictions—such as coffee, cocaine, and chocolate—was not the usual type of conquest, but a passive and embracing kind; a victory than began with the victor being devoured. *Chile* won the world in the way women win men. Even though *chiles* have a strong feminine component and property, it's a property that remains one of those cultural secrets I so often mention.

It is more common to think of *chiles* as masculine, especially in Mexico. "*Chile*" is a term very frequently applied to the masculine member. *Chiludo* means having a big "*chile*"; therefore "well hung". The *chile* is strong, it "bites". In Spanish, capsicum is not "hot": we would say a *chile* is *picante* or *picoso*. The word *pica* is an aggressive verb that describes the bite of ant or the sting of a bee, or the sauce of sarcastic, biting, *picaresco* humor. It also has the same sense of English words like "pick" and "peck", as well as the beak of a bird.

In that sense it is yet another term men apply to their sexual member, a term I readily understand; there was a period in my life when my image of male sexuality was very much like that kind of "picking"; a sharp, devastating piercing and carrying away. *"Pico"* meant to me the deadly beaks of rapine birds. I understood it by watching the *garzas*, white egrets that hunted in the marshes, wading in with emotionless eyes to watch for the chance to stab that stiff length of death into whatever careless fish swam by.

But the English concept of *chiles* having "heat" may be more accurate. *Chile* does "burn" the tongue and also has a warming fire, a burning of a nutritious kind, as all food is burned to fire our lives. One of my brothers-in-law used to eat *chiles* all day. He would even cut open sweet buns and fill them with beans and fierce *habanera chiles*, a strange Mexico City combination I could never understand. He would pack it into his mouth with one hand, using the other to wipe his brow of the sweat the *chiles* brought forth.

In Mexican cooking, *chiles* are seen more as a food than as a spice or producer of heat. But often people who treat *chiles* more as a source of fire than of taste or food value, who brag of what they can bear to eat, are the same ones who take that fire lightly and don't understand that capsaicin can be as actually dangerous as any other powerful chemical. A *chile de arbol* or a *habanero* can be fifty times more *picoso* than the bland *jalapeños* to which people are more accustomed. A raw *habanero* should be handled very carefully, even with gloves. The capsaicin can cause grave damage to the mouth or even fingers and if gets in the eyes can threaten the vision. I once bit into a small yellow *chile mazana* and its juice squirted out on my cheek, causing me a painful swelling and blistering of my entire cheek and jaw. A strong *chile* is natural chemical warfare, nothing to take lightly.

Once it is swallowed, a very *picoso chile* takes on a dominance, is in biological control. A person who is *chileado* is often offered advice and recipes, but there is little that can be done against the suffering. I would say to avoid water and beer, but take milk, yogurt or other dairy products if they are available. And to be careful, since even identical *chiles* can vary in their power.

Men joke about all this; the male symbolism, the macho ordeals. They brag of the hot *chiles* they eat, they boast of how many they have taken from their fields. But between the harvesting and the serving, the women care for those little red phalluses; dry them carefully in the sun, store them in the dark away from the damp and the insects, select them, grind them, measure them, mix them to taste, present them at the table. Men may sow the *chiles* in the soil and take them out, but it is women who make the *mole*.

If the *chile* is the primordial essence of Mexican food, then the *mole* sauce is its most graceful expression, perhaps the most traditional dish of the *cocina Mexicana*. It is also a classic of subtlety and submerging of flavors into a symphonic taste; the word *mole* means "mixture" in Nahuatl, the pre-Columbian *lingua franca* often called the "Latin of the Americas". Foreigners are familiar with *mole*, but generally a flat, simple, chocolate-dominated version. I have a book published in Mexico with recipes for *mole rojo*, *mole verde*, the classic *mole poblano*, even the yellow Oaxacan *mole* of *chile güero*. The recipes call for a dozen ingredients each, but are also simpler than the realities of good, if humble, restaurants. It is a book for modern literate people with seventy thousand pesos to spend on a book. A true *mole* is a much more complex affair.

There is a popular, though somewhat mythical, story about the creation of *mole poblano*. It tells about an eighteenth century Archbishop visiting the Convent of Santa Rosa in Puebla. The cook was unexpectedly taken ill, so the *Madre Superiora* placed an inexperienced young nun in charge of preparing a fine meal for the Archbishop—under threat of excommunication if she failed. Awed and frightened in the strange kitchen, the *monjita* prayed for guidance then started assembling a sauce as best she saw fit. Starting out with a chicken or turkey would be obvious, but how should it be sauced and seasoned? Pork fat is always a good place to start.

And what *chiles* were on hand? Sweet, mild *anchos,* raisiny *mulatos,* and dark, rich *pasillas,* of course—all common in Puebla and considered the "holy trinity" of *mole* preparation. *Chiles* would suggest tomatoes, onions and garlic. Then let's grind up some almonds and peanuts. And while the grinding stones are out, why not continue with chocolate and some squash seeds? And was it religious euphoria or merely the contents of the pantry that suggested such unorthodox ingredients as raisins and plantains? And finally, as insurance, wouldn't it be wise to spare no spice? As long as there are pepper, anis, clove, cinnamon, cumin, and sesame within reach, why leave any of them out? What could she do but throw these together in hope of heaven? Now we know her randomly chosen ingredients were blessed with a happy marriage and the story usually concludes with the Archbishop happily licking his fingers and granting the inspired apprentice a lifetime pardon for venial sins.

I assume this cute account to be apocryphal, quite aside from its ecclesiastic irregularities and the fact that *mole* was known to civilizations older than the Aztecs. I have heard an identical story of the first "chow mein" being thrown together by a dishwasher under fear of a gangster in a Chinese restaurant in New York. But there are those who enjoy the idea that great discoveries can come out of accidents or "random" events, that even the human body and mind could have been organized out of the soup of ancient seas by the exercise of co-incidence and deadly competitions. And there are other people who like the idea of ingredients cohering through divine guidance. The story of the *poblana* nun serves both tastes.

Myself, I don't even feel that such a thing as "random" truly exists. A *mole,* well understood, is in itself a strong argument against the idea. Everybody nods at the story of the little nun, but nobody believes that a great sauce is created by throwing ingredients together. Try it yourself: see if you end up with a complex sauce of hidden lights and fires or a nasty mud. A *mole* is not an accident or a triumph, it is a marriage: to happily marry distinct flavors like chocolate and *chile* is art, not science or war.

It's one thing to state an ingredient like squash seed or chocolate or raisins. It's another matter to prepare each element so that they will mix and marry their flavors. *Chiles* must be roasted and stemmed if fresh, rehydrated if dried, then cooked without boiling, then pureed. Sesame seeds must be popped like popcorn, raisins soaked, chocolate liquefied. Much of the work comes from "grinding the seeds", making a paste of the various grains, seeds, and other materials. Traditionally this was done by hand against rough stone; practically it is done by electricity in blenders. Restaurants don't do grinding by hand any more than they milk their own cows. In Mexico City there are places where *mole* ingredients are hand ground on stone *metates*, but they are places where a dish might cost forty dollars, museums for wealthy collectors of culinary experiences like Tokyo's exclusive restaurants of blowfish sushi.

Within a closer locale (and price range), I would recommend that *mole* explorers try La Casa Del Mole, where the cooks are from Puebla and recipes are inherited from generations of *poblana* grandmothers. They may use blenders instead of *molcajetes*, but there is no compromise on ingredients. They even use actual *cacao* "beans" along with the usual chocolate. All this in a simple but authentic *ambiente* for around five dollars. They also have a treat *chile aficionados* don't find everywhere, dried *chile morita* ground with garlic and almonds for sprinkling on anything that seems to demand it. The Casa also prepares an excellent "*Mixiote*"; although they bake the chicken and *chile ancho* in foil instead of the older way of wrapping it in the skin stripped off *maguey* leaves, they place pieces of the *maguey* fiber inside to give the distinctive flavor. And with my unfortunate predilection for sweets, I should mention they serve exquisite *tamales* stuffed with a raisin-pineapple-coconut paste, and a perfect mug of pineapple or guava *atole*.

Of course, it's much easier to buy prepared *moles* from big clay pots in Calimax or Gigante. And they aren't so bad, though they lack ingredients and subtlety. Easier yet is to buy canned Doña Maria paste and add chocolate and boiling water at home. I've even seen people I know adding Hershey's syrup to such packaged sauces, but naturally I wouldn't do that. Or most certainly would not admit to it.

Anyone with any interest in *chiles* should go to the Mercado Hidalgo, Tijuana's biggest market. It covers an entire block in the Zona Rio, a block south on Tenth from the traffic circle between Plaza Rio and the Tijuana Cultural Center. The Mexicoach passes right in front of it so it's a convenient side trip to a visit to the Cultural Center, there always being more than one level of culture. In addition to restaurants and tons of fresh produce of every kind, Mercado Hidalgo has huge heaps of dried *chiles*, the best selection, and the lowest prices. It's the best place to experience some of the variety of *chiles* available. There brown *chipotles*, big fat red *serranos*, the *cascabel* like dried cherries, black *teñir* and *mulato*, long *pullas* and *pasillas*, *guajillos* like transparent red plastic.

But I think the best thing is that it allows the opportunity to be in small spaces permeated with the smell and feel of *chile*. Mixed, of course with sticks of cinnamon, baskets of clove and cumin, jars of anise and other dried spices. A shopper can investigate the look and feel of dried *chiles*, learn to differentiate them. The *cascabel*, for instance rattles when shaken.

Dried *chiles* not only keep better than fresh ones, their flavors are deeper and more distinctive. Look for deep uniform color in dried *chiles*; some even glow like glass when held up to the light. Beware of fading, dust or spots, and learn to feel the slight resilience of a *chile* that has not been dried too long. And of course, check the aroma.

Avoid broken *chiles* that might have lost something of their oils, though dried *chiles* kept intact in a tight container can keep for an indefinite time. Those found in the ancient Peruvian tombs were still *picoso* after nine millennia. Dried *chiles* can be powdered and used like supermarket "chili powder" (but blended from several different types to your own taste). They can be soaked for use in Mexican salsas, strung into decorative wreaths for the kitchen, or used in traditional recipes. Or the seeds can be removed and planted; *chiles* are as easy to grow as tomatoes.

The market is heaven for serious Mexican food enthusiasts, but also for anyone with an interest in food in general. Of course, it is also merely the basic course. *Chile* fanatics breed their own *chiles* and seek out rare ones seen only in southern or remote markets. My sister Monica keeps a very comprehensive collection of *chiles* (one sniff of her kitchen remains unforgettable for life) and impresses us on occasion with rare sauces. Friends in southern states send her rarities like the blue *chile patzquaro* and even the *chihuacle negro*, an extremely rare and expensive "collectors" *chile*. It's dark, smoky flavor is the necessary ingredient for the famous black *moles* of Oaxaca. Not everyone will want to become such a connoisseur but maybe there are readers who, like myself, find it interesting to know the full variety and history of the many species. Not that history and botany will help you much when your forehead is sweating, your eyes are weeping, and your mouth feels like it's full of malignant scorpions. There is always more than one level of understanding.

These are also my reasons for writing about race and culture. Others have written about *mestizaje,* and the use of blending foods as a metaphor for blending races is not new. But for all the very noisy, very recent fashion for denigrating Columbus and the other European invaders of the Americas, it goes un-mentioned that the indigenous peoples were quite occupied with invading, conquering—and yes, enslaving each other—long before their unfortunate encounter with a civilization capable of accomplishing those things more efficiently.

There is less discussion of what the Aztecs absorbed from or imposed on the conquered Toltecs, the Toltecs on the Olmecs, the Olmecs on whatever people they conquered and enslaved. And even less on the absorption and effects of dietary customs. It is clear that much was passed from one triumphant civilization to another, but how did people's diets change during the centuries when they entered the New World from Asia? Certainly as much as the racial change from Asians to "Indians" (was Columbus so wrong, after all, to call them that?). Whoever came to Latin America, even before it was either Latin or America, started to eat *chiles*. And potatoes and corn and peanuts and chocolate.

If there is any truth behind saying that you are what you eat, you'd have to say that people who eat those things become Americans. Quite apart from race, the land makes the people its own. Those who live in the mountains become mountaineers, seacoast dwellers acquire a coastal point of view, people in the desert become desert fauna. You who are reading this might be of any race, but you are a Californian. So are those in Baja California who cannot read it. And since you are a Californian, this is not news to you about *chiles*; it is an invitation to enjoy them more completely. If you are a native of the Californias or Mexico, *chiles* are a birthright. If not, please make yourself a guest.

Because if there are any lessons in mixing, it is that lines are made to be crossed. There is very little that we are—race, color, language, culture—that can not be changed and hybridized, that cannot be taken away by the centuries of not-quite-random stirring as surely as our lesser possessions can be taken by force. When Mexicans speak of *mestizaje*, they refer to the blending of Spaniards and American natives and think of it as something of past history that has become stable and static. But in truth, the blending is not yet over.

There has been Negro blood in Mexico for a long time; since slaves were brought to the new world, slaves have escaped. There are centuries of Asian blood, especially on the west coast where ships from China traded in days when the rule of Spain extended to Manila. You can find Mexicans who look like Asiatics, Africans, Europeans, red Indians. When men of different blood come ashore, they look around them and they are looked at. The process may look random, but that's a superficial view; our human seed is designed so that the beauty of women draws the seeds of men and everyone concerned thinks they know what they are doing and why.

And now, at the border between these cities, you can see blends mixing with blends. How many generations would you have to go back to trace the pure Danish gene a suntanned California blonde from Minnesota might mingle with the pure Aztec gene of a light-skinned *Tijua* from Mexico City. This area is full of bi-lingual, bi-national *mestizos* bred by mutual attractions, often of the most superficial kind. Their seed develops differently depending upon the soil in which in falls; living only a hundred yards one side of the border or the other makes a difference we see every day but can hardly imagine. But the seed carries on without regard to those differences of a single generation, the fire handed down again and again.

If we are among those who think we know what we are doing we sometimes have to stop and ask ourselves what we are doing. Are we fusing the races of the world into a harmonic golden people. . . or scrambling our heritage into a featureless brown mud? The only thing that occurs to me is my grandmother making mole. She told me, "Keep the ingredients clean, pure and separate. Mix them as well as you can and give them time to marry. When you eat, you should be able to taste every flavor, including some new ones. Nothing should be lost or buried." And, of course, a little prayer wouldn't do any harm.

IV. FLOWERS IN THE DUST

ANTONIA

I come from very poor people, but when I was a baby a neighbor girl took care of me while my mother worked and went to the market. I think most people in Mexico have maids or servants in the house, even many of the very poor. Maybe this is not true in the United States, where people have more money. This seems strange, but maybe I just don't understand.

It seems natural that younger women with no children would help with the families of older women who have many. What else is a young, unmarried girl going to do? Maybe they get meals, or a few pesos or maybe it is just part of their obligation to their aunts or cousins. But most times if you are around a Mexican family, there will be a younger woman or even a girl of twelve years who is keeping the babies, helping with the food, sweeping the yard.

When I was in my teens I kept house for my uncle, whose wife had died. I did the same work I would have done in my father's house, but I enjoyed it more because I was in charge. The children were all younger and it was like having babies of my own. I cooked and cleaned and watched the children with nobody to boss me around. We ate better, too, because my uncle worked a syndicate job in the cane mill instead of farming like everybody else. And I had much more privacy in his house than in my own.

I was in the middle of thirteen children and we lived in three rooms with hammocks on the porch for sleeping so there was no privacy at all. In my uncle's house I was older than his six children and had certain respect and obedience from them. They called me "*Tia*", though I was really their cousin, not their aunt. I even had a little space, a sort of curtained closet that had been my aunt's, where I could hang my dresses, look in the mirror, be alone. Now, here in this country, it seems impossible that a young girl becoming a woman would not have privacy to dress up and to know her body, but then and there it seemed normal enough.

This was in Sinaloa, in a *pueblito* not far from Rosamorado. I was happy enough cleaning my uncle's house and going to school sometimes, but my friends always talked about getting married or leaving town and going someplace more exciting. You understand, ours was a town with no *zocalo*, only streets full of dust or mud: no cinema, no library, no bar, no restaurant. It is still a very boring place and if I went back there I wouldn't stay for long.

Well, I didn't see anyone I wanted to marry. The boys were all a bunch of *burros* and the boys from bigger places like Rosamorado were not to be trusted. I'll admit to being vain. My friends told me I was too pretty to stay there, that I should go where I would be appreciated by real men, have a fine life. It sounded like a good idea and I thought that if I could go somewhere bigger that men would come to me, would like a girl who looked like the girls on TV, but had small-town manners. Even my uncle told me I should go out into the world, not stay there and grow old. "Like a flower in the dust", he said. But how was I to make my way?

There was one way. Go to the border and work as a maid in a foreign household. Everyone knew about this. Every

year some of the girls would catch the bus to Tijuana or
Ciudad Juarez and try to get jobs on the other side of the frontier. Some came back to visit at *Semana Santa* with nice clothes
and money. Some never came back.

There were advertisements sometimes, looking for
young girls to come to the frontier and work in houses. I
wanted to do that, because they would pay my way. But my
mother would not allow it. She was like most of the mamas,
afraid of *poquianchismo*, slavery of white women. They would
tell us of the dangers and they would always tell the same stories; the Gonzalez sisters.

It must be thirty years now since they caught Eva
Gonzalez Valenzuela, but they talk about it like it was last
week's newspapers. The evil sisters would place announcements for work as maids in the North to lure young girls from
their homes. They fished enough girls up, three thousand they
say, but that could be an exaggeration. Here in the poor vil-
lages we have always thought that the border is paved with
gold. But instead of jobs, the girls were enslaved into prostitution. They were raped and taken to the infamous brothel in
San Francisco Rincon to be starved and beaten until they were
docile. Then they would be sold to other houses and worked
as long as they lasted. Many were killed. There were hundreds
of skeletons found buried in Maria Gonzalez' garden. I listened
to these stories with shivers of fear. I could imagine the horror
and the wicked sisters burying the poor girls at night. The
details of the raping and shaming were never made clear, but
seemed fascinating and terrifying to us. Of course this was to
frighten us from leaving home. These days everyone thinks the
border is paved in blood.

Finally my cousin Blanca made the decision to go to
Tijuana. She was pretty wild but of course even she wouldn't
travel alone so she asked me to go with her. Her argument was
that if we didn't leave when we were young we would be
trapped. Our families wanted us to stay because they didn't

want to lose us as workers and producers of more workers. She said, "If we are going to clean house, we might as well get paid for it." I thought about it and realized it was true. They wanted to trade us among themselves, to always have somebody to have children, clean the house, care for them in their old age. I begged my uncle to loan me money to go to Tijuana. I had a little money of my own and we could stay with Blanca's aunt in Tijuana, taking care of her children while she worked on the other side cleaning houses.

He gave me the money, but made me promise not to tell my mother he had given it to me. He wished me well and told me two things I never forgot. He said to be careful, that men would spoil my beauty in order to possess it. And he told me never to rely on my looks to earn my bread or I would regret it. I have been lucky, but I have seen other girls suffer for not following that advice and I thank him for it. I didn't tell my mother good-bye, just left her a letter. We caught a ride to Rosamurado and bought tickets to Tijuana. We were two very excited girls, and scared half to death.

I'll never forget stepping off the bus, the huge station full of men looking us over and *coyotes* offering us rides to Los Angeles. I was very excited and glad that I had come. But after a few days of greeting everyone and being shown around by my cousins, we were right back to spending all day watching the babies, cooking and cleaning up the house. I was reading the newspapers and seeing exciting opportunities for young women. There were jobs in factories and hotels, things I'd never thought of. There were schools to teach accounting and even computers, which fascinated me a little. But Blanca was not interested when I showed her the announcements. The truth is, I'm not sure she could even read them. She was always more interested in boys and games than in school. She said we should continue with our idea to get jobs as maids. In the United States. Well, that was a different kind of excitement and I wasn't so sure. To leave the hills for Tijuana was one thing, to leave Mexico for a strange, rich, violent country was another thing. But she insisted and did most of the work to find us jobs, while I watched the *bambinos* and read the papers and thought of myself wearing a nice dress and working with a computer in an office full of young men in smart suits.

I'll say this for Blanca, she found both of us jobs in homes in San Diego in less than a month. With the help of our aunt and a thousand of her friends, of course. That's how it works; a business that's all from mouth to mouth. There's no organization at all. The good thing is that the same position might re-open many times. Young girls move on or get married or get homesick or make enough money to go back home. So they give word to their friends and the news passes around. And maybe friends of the *patrón* ask where they could find a maid and the *señora* asks if there is a sister who wants a position.

We telephoned people we had heard of, or that our cousins knew. Lots of the people we talked to spoke Spanish, many were Mexican citizens living across the line. But international phone calls are expensive and very difficult to place from the public long distance booths. So much information in this business is carried by mouth or passed hand to hand on scraps of paper. There's a huge net of relatives, friends, inquiries, whispers, lost phone messages, old women carrying tales.

I saw all this confusion and thought that there must be some way to organize it all, to bring the girls to one place and charge a fee to connect them with jobs. But I realized it would never work. You could not place announcements on the United States side because it is illegal. It would be possible here in Tijuana but how would you collect your commission or finder's fee once the girls had crossed over? Well, you could threaten to report them if they didn't pay, but really that would be unthinkable. Americans don't understand how much Mexicans hate the Border Patrol. They are always drawn as huge, cruel brutes with sharp, dripping teeth like wolves and

73

massive weapons to massacre Mexican *mojados*. Even people who have never been near the border hate the *migra*, just like people who have never met mafiosos or Gestapos hate them. You could not betray a person to them for money or nobody would come to you again. Everyone would hate you, as though you had betrayed Jews to the Nazis. Besides, the girls make very little money, maybe only two hundred dollars a month apart from their room and food. It's too bad, but there would be no way to have an agency. Maybe with the Free Trade Treaty. Who knows? Mexico is changing. The world is changing.

Once we had positions, we had to find a way to get across the border to claim them. Our future *patrones* were not willing to smuggle us across in their own cars, which would have been the safest way for us. We would have to report to work by our own efforts. We had heard the usual terrible stories of difficult crossings through dangerous terrain, of people being betrayed and sold, of people being robbed and raped and killed. After all people go through to arrive at the border, the last few meters of the trip are the worst part and we were afraid to make any move at all. As it came about, we were lucky and contacted an excellent *pollero* who offered to take us across as easily as we could cross a street in the downtown. I'd heard of illegals being called *pollos*, but hadn't heard the crossing guides called *polleros*, as though they were selling us. They also used to call them *coyotes*, which sounds even worse to the ears of the "chickens".

It is a big business in Tijuana, of course. You are constantly being solicited to pay for passage, especially when you look like recently arrived *campesinas* like Blanca and I. In fact, it's the way we met Javier, he was complimenting me at a popsicle parlor where we had taken the children for a treat. He was trying to get me to talk to him, to seduce me, really. . . but in a way that was not embarrassing. Blanca ignored him (she was probably jealous). He was a good-looking man of maybe twenty-four years; well-built, well-groomed, very shiny hair, and a cute smile. He dressed like a border cowboy, but with style and expense. He was wearing black jeans and boots and a Stetson when we met, American sun glasses, a red bandanna at his throat, and a red denim jacket open to the waist. No shirt. And of course he was quite dashing, a man of the world who made his money through danger. I let him flatter me without answering him. I'll admit to having been very vain of my looks back in Sinaloa but in Tijuana I was not so special. Just one more country girl with an Indian accent and unfashionable clothes. I was enjoying his attention.

When he said he was a *coyote*, Blanca became more interested and started talking business (with some attentions of her own). He told us he was very good at his business, that we could cross safely with him without fear or discomfort. He said I could wear high heels and a long skirt if I wanted. Then he winked at me. Blanca asked for his address, but he gave it to me. Blanca's uncle verified Javi's "credentials" and references for us. He asked questions of people around Colonia Libertad, even the police. He even went over and had a drink with Javi himself. He told us that any crossing is a risk, but Javi seemed the safest he'd heard of. He wanted three hundred dollars from each of us, which my uncle said was a high price, but fair enough if he was as good as he said. Blanca's aunt loaned her the money and mine would be paid by my *patron* when Javi "delivered" me. In return, I would work the first month for them without pay. This had all been arranged through the network of calls and whispers and customs.

On the night we were to go, I was terrified. If my cousin hadn't been going with me I wouldn't have left the house. We met Javi at La Dichosa, a large open-air taco stand in Lower Libertad. I couldn't eat a thing from nervousness and fear. There were eight of us, five men in their twenties and another girl, one of the men's fiancée. She was older than we were, maybe eighteen years, but seemed glad to see us come to the table. Javi had told us there would be at least one other woman along on that trip, which was why we'd decided on that particular night. We waited in La Dichosa, everyone nervous, until after midnight. Meanwhile, Javi was taking us, one by one, to another table and talking to us. It was his final check that everyone had the money or somebody to pay when they arrived. He didn't care which. That was one thing that made me trust him more—if he'd insisted on having cash, I'd have been afraid that he wanted to rob us.

I was surprised when he waved me over to his table. He knew I had no money. He had an American partner who checked each person who was supposed to pay his fee on the other side. He was making a final check, asking each person again who would pay, where they lived, maybe some detail his partner had learned when talking to the ones who would pay. He said, "I am a very careful *coyote*, which is why my *pollos* always come to the roost safely."

But he didn't ask me about the people. He looked at me and told me I could go across for free if I wanted to, keep the three hundred. I asked him how, but I already knew. He said his services were free to his special friends and loved ones, that he would like me to be loved by him. I should have told him no, but I was silly then and more of a coquette. I asked him how I could trust him to keep his part of the bargain, once I had done my part. He smiled at me as though I had agreed, touched my hand, and told me that it was not necessary to trust him. He would deliver me across the border first, with faith that I would then complete the bargain in a nice hotel he knew in San Ysidro, with a bottle of champagne and some nice lingerie he would buy for me. I felt like I had been trapped by my own foolishness and just shook my head until he started laughing. He said, "That's why we call you chickens, you know. Because of the way you shake your heads and run away from the rooster." I was red in the face and felt ashamed and stupid, but he told me I was all right and called for a guitarist to come play for me, a tribute to my beauty he said. The guitarist played "Volver, Volver, Volver". It means "Return, return, return" a very sentimental Mexican song and it affected all of us who were about to leave our country. Javi leaned over to whisper to me. He said, "When you return, come and love me," and kissed my ear. I went back over to sit by the other girls without looking at his face. He just laughed.

Finally a big red and black taxi came and we all got in. Javi asked me to sit up front between him and the driver, but of course I didn't. I sat in the back with my cousin and told her what Javi had said to me. She acted very shocked, but I saw her giving him an eye and realized she probably would have done it. Maybe even without the discount. He was not the sort of man one meets in our little *puebulucho*. Not at all.

The taxi took us up Otay Mesa, near the University. We seemed to be just driving around, moving towards the airport. Nobody was talking except Javi and the *taxista*. They were talking about the very latest in information about the movements of the *migra*. My impression was that they had a very special spot and were using it only with small groups to protect it from discovery. They seemed very relaxed and were sharing a bottle of Tequila.

Everything seemed to depend on when two *migra* cars would go to a store for coffee, which they usually did at the same time every night. We were driving without headlights and stopped several times while Javi and the driver stared across into the dark and said things that made no sense to me. Then we entered a short alley that led to a fence. I looked at it, wondering if I could climb it. Javi got out, went over to the fence and just opened it up like a door.

The fence had been cut very straight and hooked on nails on the south side of the pole so the cuts could not be seen from the other side. Javi motioned us out of the taxi and through the opening in the fence. The driver was closing it behind us. Javi told us, very casually, to just walk behind him and keep quiet. But if he said, "Drop," we were to fall flat on the ground and if he said, "Back," we should run back to the fence and the *taxista* would be waiting to open it for us. But there was no need. We walked across the weeds like strolling through a park. And just when we reached a highway a van pulled over, Javi opened the door and we jumped in and drove off. Javi smiled at me and said, "See? You could have worn your high heels." I realized that we were in the United States, that I was an outlaw.

We drove to three different places, just late night stores, and men got out and paid Javi or someone waiting would pay. The van driver, who never said anything to us, was an American and probably the same partner that checked on those who paid, because he looked very closely at the men who came up to meet the van, and waited until he had heard them speak before he said anything. They would offer the gringo money, he would point at Javi, they would pay him. Then one of the young men would get down from the van and go away with him. One very mean-looking Mexican man paid for the young couple. He gave Javi money without speaking, Javi took it without counting it.

At the Vons store in Bonita where I was to meet my new *patrones*, Javi got out with me and walked me over to a parked car, a huge blue Cadillac. The people in the car looked like good people to me, a middle-aged couple that you could tell had been married a long time by the way they sat. As we walked up, Javi told me it was my last chance to save three hundred dollars and have the thrill of my life. I glanced at him and shook my head, but I smiled. He wasn't a bad type, really. He smiled back and said, "Come look for me when you grow up. When you return." Actually, I found him very attractive. He must be one of the very best *coyotes* and we were very lucky to have found him.

He took money from the man in the car, counted it, then told me, "Get in, go with them. They just bought you for a month, a year, who knows how long. For what I'd have given you for a single night." I told him he wasn't a very good businessman after all. He laughed and walked back to the van and drove away. I got in the back seat of the Cadillac and the lady turned around and smiled at me. She said, "*Bienvenidos*," then she kept on talking to me, but I couldn't understand her. I felt like I'd jumped off a bridge and was washing down the river. It was two weeks before Christmas. I had just turned sixteen.

My *patrones* are very fine people and treat me very well, almost as if I were a relative and not a stranger from another country who does not even speak their language. I have a comfortable room with my own television and bath and am free to move and eat from their kitchen. The *señora* has learned some Spanish and is always trying to learn more. She also encourages me to learn English, but I find it very difficult. I feel at home in their house, except for having nobody to really talk to. To tell you the truth, it is not that different from living with my uncle or Blanca's aunt, except I am earning money. They pay me three hundred dollars a month. In dollars. This is a great amount of money and I never spend any for food or soap or any of those things. The oldest daughter is my age and sometimes gives me or loans me clothes. So I save most of what I earn.

I am given two weeks of vacation each year and could use it to go home for a visit, but then I would have to cross the border again. Maybe I will go this year. I'm sure Javi could bring me back across, but I don't know if I want to see him. I am too young to marry and too old to play dangerous games with men like him. The truth is, I don't know if I want to go back there. It was not such a happy place for me, just a dirty little mud hole. I would like to use my vacation to travel and know this country, but I am afraid I would be caught and deported. I usually spend my free time in local Mexican places with Blanca and other girls who work in houses.

We have rented an apartment together, eight or ten of us, I don't really know how many. All friends of friends. We share the rent, which is only thirty dollars each, and have a place where we can to go on our free days. We have parties there, invite boys from Chula Vista. I keep some nice clothes there in case I want to go out. Blanca and some of the girls date a lot and the apartment gives them a place to be picked up and taken home. You couldn't have a boy call on you at the home where you work. Of course nobody likes to do housework on their free days, but we keep it clean enough. We have a stereo and television and kitchen, but only furniture the landlord lends us. He is a Mexican and likes us. Most of his tenants are illegals because he asks no questions. And if people come and ask, he answers no questions.

We have to be quiet when we have fun. It seems strange in this country to be young and have money but have to enjoy it carefully. If we enjoy ourselves enough to attract attention we could lose it all. Sometimes it's like living as a spy in foreign movie. But one of the girls has an older sister who also came here *mojada* like us but now is married and lives here legally. She says there is not so much difference in things here. She told us about walking in Chapultepec Park on Sundays and all the young maids would walk together in twos, with their eyes down. Very careful. She worked there in Mexico City as a maid for several years before coming here. It was the same thing, even without the border. Young poor girls from the country would come to the big city to work in the fine homes of the rich people. There were dangers in the city and they had to behave carefully. But they didn't want to go back to living on some miserable little rancho. It's no different from what we are doing now.

I've spent a week of vacation right there in the apartment, laughing and drinking with the other girls if they are there, maybe going to a shopping plaza or the cinema if somebody has a boyfriend with a car and good English. I like being in the apartment alone; just fooling around, listening to the radio, smoking cigarettes on the bed. I've never had my own house, but I can imagine it there. Doing what I want, walking around naked, singing in the shower, dropping ashes on the floor, dancing in front of the mirror. I like laying around in the bubble bath and drinking coffee, but only if there's nobody around. At such times it's a long, long way from where I was born. Blanca wants only to marry a boy who is a citizen and get a place of her own. (And get pregnant and fat, clean house and raise children.) I'm not so sure. Maybe I will go to school, learn English and computers. I like the life you can have here. I just haven't learned how I can make it my own place. But I've only been here three years. I'm still learning a lot of things.

As far as working goes, it is not bad. In some ways it was harder to keep house in my village. Most of our houses were made of posts with palm thatch roofs, which would get full of spiders and scorpions. The walls were split cane, nailed to the posts with bottle caps to keep the nails from tearing through. It was like looking through mini-blinds and the dust came right in whenever the goats or burros or trucks went by. The floor was dirt and chickens would run through the house and the pigs would try to lie on the patios under the roof. The light was a propane lantern that made smoke. So things got dirty quickly and there was no water heater. We bathed in the river and heated dish water on the stove. We carried the propane tanks several kilometers to get them filled. It sounds strange to me after living here, but it's common enough in Mexico. In the countryside.

On the other hand, there was no need to wash or wax the floors; I would use a broom to sweep the inside, then the patios, then the yard. Spills just soaked into the floor. There were not so many dishes or things to clean. There were maybe three towels in the house: in the house I work now there are dozens and they take a long time to wash and dry. You have to spend a lot of time with the clothes dryer, instead of just hanging things on a rope. That was something I could make the children do. Same way, watching the children was easier in Mexico because I was making them work.

In a way it was less bother there. Here, after meals I put the food that remains into the refrigerator. I have to wrap it up and put it in plastic dishes. There is a lot of it. There is a lot of garbage to take out and it takes more plastic bags and moving things from one plastic container to another. It is easier just to throw it out the window for the goats to eat, let the old man come around and pick out the cans. There are hours of work to keep a bathroom all shiny, to keep even a toilet shined and free of odor. The first time I was in this house, that was most amazed me—the bathroom. The bowl and toilet and tub are all the same color of ceramic. The floor is carpeted—even the toilet seat is carpeted. One whole wall is mirror—you can study yourself using the toilet. Everything is silvery and shiny. A fan comes on to blow away smells, a red light in the ceiling warms you when you get out of the shower. There are mountains of clean, soft towels in beautiful colors. You can drop toilet paper straight into the toilet and it goes down without ever stopping up the plumbing. There is even a bottle in the toilet to turn the water blue to match the walls. There is a rack for magazines to read while you are there, even a telephone. I found it even more marvelous than the kitchen. I would spend all my time in there if it were my house, maybe put the television in there. But it's strange, too; like having a shrine to the basest of bodily functions. And it takes hours to keep it clean.

The kitchen is also incredible. Everything is electric, there are no flames. So it isn't so hot to cook in the summer, but neither is it nice and warm in there. There are tables and chairs in the kitchen but nobody ever eats there. I don't understand that. But during parties, everyone ends up standing in the kitchen, even though there are large beautiful salons like in a movie or *Casas* magazine. There is a radio that's always on, usually on Radio Latino. There are small electrical things to do everything; open cans, make popcorn, peel vegetables, make pancakes, cook a single hamburger, melt cheese. My *patrona* was surprised to see me peel a potato with a knife. She showed me a special tool for doing it. Now, I can barely peel vegetables and my friends laugh at me—a paid United States housekeeper who can't even peel a cucumber. But they can't pat tortillas like my mama could, either—they buy them rolled out by machines. When my *patrona* cooks, she uses dozens of dishes and pans and tools. Of course, all these marvels must be cleaned and put away. And everything must be sprayed with poisons and germ-killers and insecticides. This is in a house with doors sealed by rubber, with no cracks in the walls, with floors covered by a single piece of linoleum, where the windows have screens and are never opened because of the air-conditioning.

It's a dream world really, like the advertisements on television. Everything snowy white, everything soft, everything new, everything bright. The *señora* watches Mexican television sometimes, to improve her Spanish. She is learning well for a person of her years. She has asked me a few times about the commercials on the *novelas* she watches. They always have tall, blond people in expensive houses wrapping blue-eyed babies up in wonderfully white cloths. She knows that very few people in Mexico live like that and has asked me several times why people accept this, how they could believe in a commercial where things are so unrealistic. I tell her that everyone knows that television is fantasy, not a real place or real world. Of course things are beautiful and perfect— it's television. Who'd want to buy soap or toilet paper if they showed a lot of ugly *negros* using it in filthy shacks? She doesn't understand. I believe that Americans think what the see on television is real, more real than their own lives. They want to live in Dallas or Dynasty and think they can get there if they buy the right things. Maybe that's the famous American Dream. I don't know. For the rest of the world the American Dream is just to live in America. I live here now. So I know it's real.

GABRIELA

I've been working in the United States for almost fifteen years now and the entire matter of cross-border working is completely misunderstood and misrepresented. On this side, that is. In Mexico people understand it perfectly. It would be a pleasure to explain a few things to you. I warn you, I'm a woman of opinions.

One thing, it's important to realize that many of the Mexican day workers in San Diego, people who cross the border every day with *micas* or *pasaportes* are just as illegal as the "wetbacks" that come across at night and live in orchards. The permit I carry, that most domestics carry, is only good for coming across the border for a day. For shopping or things like that. And not every day—it is not a green card or work paper. So I am working illegally. But there are so many of us. Almost any border resident can obtain a card like mine from the consulate. You fill out the famous "Form Thirty" and prove you live in the frontier area and have a job and home and aren't trying to jump out of the country.

All my illegal status means is that I must get up early and cross very carefully. I dress as though going to shop, I carry an empty shopping bag. I have money in my purse. I approach the lines carefully, watching without appearing to be watching. If I went in front of the same guard several days consecutively, they would start to remember me. So I choose my line and do nothing to draw attention. I keep underclothes and hygiene supplies at the houses where I work. Some women sneak across a pair of panties or toothbrush in their purse, but some times these are found. It is possible to lose the card, to be barred from legally crossing in order to illegally work. This is a great hardship.

However, it isn't incurable—there is a great black market in papers and cards. If you look like I do, a Mexican women of Indian appearance but with the clothes and manner of a worker, you can walk to the Jack in the Box restaurant in San Ysidro near the trolley, and men will approach you trying to sell you false identification. It's like a farmer's market for forgers and thieves. For the price of one thousand dollars I've been offered a *pasaporte* that would pass any inspection. (By *pasaporte* I mean a visit card, an official United States diplomatic passport would sell for much more.) A friend of mine bought some documents there. For one of them she walked across the street to the pay parking lot where the forger had a camera apparatus in the back of a van. He took Polaroid pictures of her in the van and she had her papers within minutes. The police have secret agents that patrol the area, but they are apparently very obvious and almost nobody is ever arrested. When there are police agents in the Jack in the Box, the paper sellers are in Burger King or the Greyhound station. Everyone knows where they are except the police.

So, I walk into this country legally, then work illegally. Just as Americans work, hunt, and fish illegally in Mexico. There are thousands that do the same, a taxless economy that must involve millions of dollars. There is no mystery about why people do it. The pay for even menial jobs in this country is very high compared to the pay in Tijuana, breathtakingly higher than in the interior of Mexico. Personally, I like the pay and find the work educational.

Maybe by now you realize I am not illiterate. Let me tell you about myself. People look at me, riding the trolley, sweeping floors in somebody's house, and they see a middle-aged Mexicana; dark-skinned, stocky, flat-faced. An ignorant peasant, right? Actually, I'm not that typical peasant at all. I'm not sure that "typical" person actually exists. I very well educated and intelligent. I read books. I mean real books. I see what people read in the houses I clean. Other than professional books, they read popular trash. One family I work for reads nothing but the TV guide. Nothing wrong with that. But I have a hard time finding books to read. The Tijuana library is a joke. The bookstores are expensive and there is no selection. The Salamanca I've been reading has passed through the hands of four of my friends. Four friends that went to the University with me by the way, who are also Licentiates in Social Work. None of us are social workers. One is married, one sells jewelry from office to office. Two of us clean houses. Tijuana is a very expensive city. I could not live and raise my family on what my degree would bring me. Cleaning houses I make almost one hundred dollars a day.

That is what attracted me to the field in the first place. I was careless and had a daughter with no husband to support us. I needed money and heard people talking about making very nice money on the other side of the border. Doing what almost any woman (at least any Mexican woman) is taught to do from childhood—clean the house. I had a card to cross (almost any University student can have one) so I started crossing, answering newspaper ads for maids. In a few weeks I had jobs lined up. Plenty of money.

Look. . . how can I explain this? It's important. You understand that most Americans, especially writers and teachers and social workers and other well-to-do people, think of personal service like this as low-class, as poverty, as a shame. They act like it shouldn't exist, want to think of it as racism and imperialism and colonialism and all those tired old words from the nineteen twenties. But when you talk to people who actually work cleaning houses, all you hear is how much money they're making, what a good thing it is. Every day people in Tijuana ask me if I know of houses that they or their daughters can clean.

I'm sure you've heard rumors that there are rich women living up in neighborhoods like Cachos and Cumbres who drive Mercedes, but clean houses on the other side. The rumors are true, though such women seldom admit it. I drove across the border in a Thunderbird four days a week with a woman who lives in a fine house right beside the Town and Country golf course. She was divorced and wanted to support the image of her fine house and her parties in designer gowns so she tied a rag around her head and did housework.

There was another reason I worked in houses, and why I continued instead of trying to advance a career in Tijuana. I was a socialist in the University, like most Mexican intellectuals. Like many American intellectuals, too, I suppose. But when I left, instead of marrying some lawyer or working for the government, I became a worker. I felt that any Marxist should experience actually being a worker. Most of my Marxists companions adored the "proletariat" but would rather have talked with a rabid dog than an actual *obrero*. Working led me to abandon my leftist beliefs and "convert" to a faith in capital, in the middle class, in the bourgeoisie. That's what almost all workers everywhere actually want—to be bourgeois and have some money invested for their old age.

By now I've come to like the work. I like working with my hands, simple repetitive work that leaves my mind free to think. Maybe vacuuming a floor would be boring for an uncultured person, but for me it is a place to think my own thoughts. You've heard, "Work is Freedom." It's very true for me. It's not my life, but it makes my life possible. And the work I do leaves my mind freer than working in some office. I wear what I want, I believe what I want. I am doing what I want. I am very well off.

I say well off. What do you think? I own my own house in Colonia 20 de Noviembre, not a fashionable neighborhood, but safe and convenient. I never work on Saturday afternoon or Sunday—those are days to spend with my family. I have a fifteen-year-old daughter and have also taken in two of my sister's children, a boy of seven years and a girl of five. My sister is recently divorced by the *pendejo* she married. Girls in our family are seen to be idiotically passionate when younger, then recover their mentality later in life. I send the children to Colegio Mentor, a very good private school.

I could easily afford to own a car, and friends who earn less than I do have them, but I don't. There is no need. To go to work I walk to the corner and within twenty minutes a collective taxi comes by and takes me to the downtown for twelve hundred pesos, maybe sixty cents "in English." For thirty cents more, a bus takes me to the border, where I walk across and catch the trolley or the "Amarillo y Rosa" bus, depending on where I'm going. Sometimes I clean a house or two and go home, other times I stay a two or three days in a house, doing full service. You know; cooking, laundry, children, maybe serving at a party.

I develop strong ties with the people I work for. Especially with the children. I would describe my clients as average American families, as near as I can tell. They look like and live like the families on American television. The Bundys, the Cosbys. I watch American television. As I say, I find things educational. I like these people, love them in time. I think anyone who spends a great deal of time in a home with anyone comes to love them. And maybe more when the time is spent serving, doing intimate things in the home.

When I speak of the home. . . you know, the Spanish word *hogar* does not mean "home" like it's used in English. In Mexico you can't sell "homes", you can't go "home" to a single apartment. *Hogar* is the hearth, a home of people, non-material things that go on between those people. This is, more than anything, what I study now, what I think about, what I live. I learn a great deal from these families, from talking to "my" people.

From what I have seen, and from what I hear, it is most common in this world to have maids. Don't laugh, I may be just a third world woman, but I talk to people. A man I work for was a ship commander, and lived all over the world. He always had women working in his house, sometimes cooks and gardeners. He told me that in the Filipinas and Japan and Panama it is like it is in Mexico, almost all families have servants or housekeepers or baby-sitters. He is from the South of the United States, from Carolina. He said he was raised by a black woman, that his children were raised by Asiatic women. He said his childhood friends, even though some are very racist, remember loving those black women, remember them almost as much as their mothers. I think it makes sense that anywhere there are families there will be a woman to help, and that she will have a girl to help her. It seems very natural.

One thing that makes me really angry is that people think I should be ashamed to work in another woman's house, to work with my hands, to clean things. There is nothing wrong with this work. If Americans believe that, fine, it makes more work for Mexicans. But I resent it when people think I'm some sort of slave, who does bad work because there is no choice. A man I work for, a social worker, showed me some pictures that some artists had done. Well, it wasn't very good art, but it said, "San Diego is America's Plantation" and had pictures of Mexicans working in chains. He explained it to me, and was surprised that I got angry.

Who are these people to say I am a prisoner? My life is my own. I am lucky to be able to come here and make as much money as I do, more than strong men make in Mexico. It's hard, but I choose to work hard. Why are they saying Mexicans are hired out of racism? Mexicans do the job better, American people don't want to do it. We are hard workers, honest people, trustworthy. We are handy because of our situation. Why should there be shame or negative propaganda? It works well for both parties. Who are these people who try to paint it negative? Artists, that's who. What do they know about work? They are like the Communists, always with their posters, always ready to save the people even when nobody wants to be saved. Save people to be true slaves. Are they offering me money? Are they saying I should not work here? That I should get more money? Ridiculous. I hardly speak English. I'm extremely lucky to be getting the money

I get now. And I am treated better in this country than I would be in my own.

Yes, that is true and anybody who works here knows it. In Mexico they call a house servant, *gata*, a very rude term. There, the *gata* would never be allowed to eat with the family: they are treated like menials, in some places almost like animals. There is a more democratic attitude here, many people here welcome maids to the table, treat them like family. I have eaten Thanksgiving dinner at the table with my employers every year I have worked here. I never hear of girls being mistreated here.

Well, I have heard of young women being sequestered into service—imprisoned in the basement and forced to work without pay. But do you know, every time it turns out the kidnapper was a Mexican—like that *chilango* on TV who was forcing that girl to free labor. And of course there is sexual harassment. I suppose you could call that mistreatment. I don't think of it that way myself. Anything other than physical force, that is. It doesn't hurt anybody; it's something a girl learns to deal with in life.

But a young girl living in the house, it's harder. Of course it's not uncommon for the men to get involved with the girls, maybe pay them. See, I can tell you were thinking only of a man forcing himself on a girl, but it's not always the man who thinks of these things first, as is often the case in life. You find this a lot. Oh, there are sexual traps here as well as in Mexico. I'm sure there are in the whole world. But it is not like in Mexico, where a girl must protect herself every minute. I've had American men I work for try to talk about sex. I just tell them, "You know, I don't like this conversation." I walk away. That's the end. None of them ever followed me or touched me. Some of them have never even looked at me in that way. In Mexico every single man would look at you like that, every one would at least press up close and try to seduce you.

I was surprised at first by the way American men approached me. Talk. They talk. They ask the questions without really asking them. I refuse and they look ashamed. It must be the way here. A Mexican man would step into the maid's room, lock the door and demand her. Maybe he would threaten to fire her or disgrace her if she did not give in—he would not accept any form of rejection. She'd be afraid to scream, afraid of the wife. Lots of girls are afraid of the woman of the house, that he'll say she was trying to get him to do it for money and she will fire the girl or beat her. It's a lot better here; if anybody touches you, they're in trouble. But down there it's hard for the girls. They're young, know nothing of law, nothing of love, of men. They're afraid of the wives because they're still afraid of their own mothers.

So it is almost inevitable for Mexican maids to become sexual toys for the men of the house. In fact, it's really an institution. There's even a word for it: *gatear*. It means to seduce the servant girls, the *gatas*. This is the way young Mexican men are supposed to initiate themselves into their manhood—on young Indian girls who work in their houses. Of course, their fathers have broken the girls in first. The little sex comics have cartoons about that joke every week. It's expected, really. So of course being a maid in Mexico is like a badge of sexual servitude. Many women won't admit it.

Mexican men are so sexually aggressive, they can't permit themselves to leave a girl under their roof unmolested. They'd be dangerous around a dog in heat. There's a saying, "A broom with a skirt would be a woman to them." When I was fourteen I was baby-sitting after school for my schoolteacher in Tijuana and he asked me to have sex with him, wanted to put me in an apartment. I told him to forget it. He was saying, "Nothing is going to happen, you won't get pregnant, I'll take care of you." And I was one of his students.

It is much easier here. But I have to tell you, I don't think women respect this as much, these half-hearted seduc-

91

tions that go nowhere. These men seem weak to me. Very nice and easy to deal with, though. I respect the men who don't try to take advantage of me. American women have a much easier life with their men, I think. But they divorce more, don't they? Anyway, it is much nicer and safer for a young girl to work in an American home than a Mexican one. But still; girls are girls, men are men.

And women, let me tell you, are women. I could do other things than clean houses and cook. But I like woman's work, it comes naturally to me. My mother trained me to do these things so I could make a good home for my husband and children. Now they are job skills. Like Mafalda's friend Susanita says in the comic strip, I'm not one of those effeminates who wants to do a man's job. I'm not afraid of hard work. The longer I live here in the United States, the less I understand the attitude towards women's jobs. Leaders of women's movements depreciate the jobs women do and glorify men's jobs. Why? And manual labor is also looked down on for some reason, as if it were dehumanizing to work with the body. They want to eliminate it. People pay more attention to the body here, as a sexual and vanity thing, but working with the body has no prestige. Women seek "professional" men, men who work at desks. It's considered better to sit at a desk all day than to build a house or tend a garden or lay bricks. Then, after work, everybody drives their cars to a gymnasium to try to have the body of a physical performer.

Service is looked down on, like some class of slavery. Yet who does not serve somebody? Most people work for wages doing something so somebody else will not have to do it. Those who are self-employed have even stricter service relationships with clients. I am self-employed myself, when you think of it. All it means is having more than one master.

What I do is natural work, very basic to life. In Mexico this is recognized, it used to be said that Mexicans live our lives to the rhythm of a woman patting dough into tortillas. I work in the home. I am a woman, I naturally feel more comfortable in the home. There are those who say different, but in fact women produce children, produce homes, are more oriented to the home by their biology and spirit. Yes, spirit. I am not a Marxist anymore, no longer a materialist. The reason there is so much controversy about women and men these days, why so many stupid things are being said, is because people no longer recognize normal sexual nature. This is because people, especially the rich, pampered academicians and writers who say stupid things are divorced from nature and live in fantasy worlds. Any farm child knows that male animals have different attitudes and spirits than female animals. A male pig, a male horse, a male fowl—they have their maleness. People in suits and deodorant who live in cars and glass cubes think people are not animals, that we are equations or technical problems that can be manipulated. It's not true. Marxism tried to pretend that people have no inner spirit, that they have no individual nature, that they don't need to control their own financial destiny. See what happened. Forget that people are animals and watch what happens. Women are foolish to try to cut themselves off from the home because it is truly the position of greatest power on the planet. Personal power, political power, healing power.

The home is not a building, it is a series of rituals. I saw a program about Japan; to make a cup of tea is a ceremony almost like a religion. I can understand that. Cooking, washing dishes, cleaning the children's clothes; really, these are sacred things. But here nobody wants to do them. You buy a machine, you hire somebody, you send your kids off to be raised by somebody else. And why? To have more time to do something more important than living life. To have more time to watch television. I have had dozens of families here. I have watched children grow up, get Christmas cards from many children, hear gossip and news from dozens of families. I've lived many, many lives here just working as a maid, being the one who keeps the house. I believe that some of these people have led no life at all. They'd paid me to do it for them.

CARMELA

I started cleaning other people's homes for a very good reason. I had no other choice. I was happily married with three kids, living in a nice house in El Mirador, working with my church, trying to lead a decent life. Then one day I came home and found my husband's wedding ring lying on top of the television. He just took it off and walked out.

I didn't see him again for over four years. Then he just showed up, told me he wanted the kids, and called me a whore because I had married another man. Even though he left me for another woman and was still with her. I spent four hard years trying to feed those kids with no help from him, then he wanted to take them away from me. It was only through Christian spirit that I kept from hating him. Hating is a sin because it harms you as much as the person you are hating. It was hard, but I learned to think of those times, of that man, as teaching me patience and faith.

I remember the worst, the lowest I ever got. It was in a very cold winter, it was even snowing in Tijuana. He had left me pregnant and I was walking through the cold with my youngest child and two big bags of groceries, struggling to get up the hill to the house. And who passes by but my husband's new woman, driving his new Topaz. When I got up to the house she was waiting in the car with the heater and radio going. She rolled down the window to tell me my husband wanted the children to come to his house for Christmas. Then she drove away. I went in the house and put up the groceries then I got down on my knees and prayed that I would learn, that I would not become bitter or teach my children to hate. I knew that we would survive. God may try us, but he does not abandon us. I never said a bad a word to my children about their father. Well, almost never. I learned to forgive him and it has made a great difference in my heart. Forgiveness is not just an act or an attitude, it must be learned and practiced.

Finally a man asked me to marry him and move to Chula Vista. I wasn't terribly in love with him, but I thought it was the best thing for my family. After five years he left me, too. He wanted a younger woman, to have children of his own. I never saw him again and don't want to. It was much easier to forgive him. Maybe because I had learned, maybe because I didn't care as much and knew I could take care of myself and my kids.

All those years alone I supported my children by cleaning houses. It was the only thing I knew how to do, the only thing I'd ever done. I never feel bad having to work, even when it's hard and the hours are long. I am never ashamed to work. I thank God I have this way to feed my children. The first time I was left alone, in Tijuana, I lived with my family until I had my youngest daughter, then I came to the American side every day to clean houses. I was helping a friend, cleaning a house one day to give her time off, helping her serve new customers so we could make more money. She was getting old and tired of all the traveling and cleaning, so I took over most of her business. She would still come one day a week because she was very close to a family. Whenever she talked about quitting, the children would cry. Even the wife would cry. She used to say, "What will they do without me? That big house? I've run it for nine years."

There is not too much to tell about cleaning houses. You clean the house. The only interesting thing is the people. The children come home and you have something for them to eat and drink, they tell you about their day. That part is simple, too. Like being a mother. If you know it, there is no need to explain. If not, there is no way to explain. Children are children. It doesn't matter what they are wearing or what they like to eat or what games they play or what language they speak.

Sometimes I would be alone with people's children for a whole day, or noon until after dark. I learned from being with different children, children I couldn't talk to so easily because of the language. My own children have turned out well, in spite of losing two fathers. Maybe it's because I learned from others. Of course, much of time my own children were watched by my mother or nieces.

In Mexico most people have a housekeeper or cook or something. Almost everybody has a baby-sitter. Even when I was poor, I had a girl to look after the kids. Now I clean houses for a living but I have a girl who lives in my house. See, I'm actually low income even though I make good money per hour. I have five children and a big house. But I have a baby-sitter who lives in my house. I pay her one hundred dollars a week and she doesn't have to pay for rent or food. I give her clothes, shampoo, those everyday things. She cleans the house and keeps an eye on the kids. She is from Mexico, doesn't speak English. She's illegal. She came up from Jalisco and called me up one day. I get a lot of calls because I've had five housekeepers. I drove her across the border in Tecate in the trunk of my car under a pile of cleaning supplies. We're pretty close and my kids love her. They'd rather be alone with her than me, I think, because she spoils them.

She looks at my house the way I looked the first time I went into a big mansion in La Jolla. She wants to meet marry a local man and get married, live here in the United States. One thing I tell her, you can't count on a man to make you happy and take care of you. You have to be ready to get by on your own, to be happy by yourself. She doesn't believe me: she's seventeen.

I made a lot of money working across the border. Sometimes fifty dollars a day which was a lot of money in Tijuana at the time. But I was lonely and tired of working all the time and glad to marry a man I met in the United States. What I remember most in those days wasn't working. You don't remember scrubbing the same bathtub or soup dish every week. I always think of riding the trolleys and buses to work. There are certain times on certain buses in San Diego when everybody on board is a domestic going to work or back home. It's almost like a club where everyone speaks a special language and understands everyone else. You get to know people. The Friday night trolley, the late bus down from North Park, the Saturday morning bus to La Jolla. Quiet rides, but in good company.

Now it's different. I am an American citizen (the only thing my second husband couldn't take away with him). I speak pretty good English. I'm not really a housekeeper or servant anymore, I'm more like a contractor for cleaning houses. I come, I clean, I get paid. After all these years, I wouldn't say cleaning houses is my favorite thing to do with my time. But it's not the worst work and I'm used to it. Where else could I make this kind of money? If I work fast, I can make up to twenty dollars an hour. I probably average fifteen dollars an hour. This for someone with no schooling or training. I come into a house during the daytime and I do everything. The dishes, the laundry, the floors. . . . When I leave the house there is no dirt left. I charge thirty-five for a one bedroom house, up to one hundred for a big three-bedroom. So it is not hard for me to make one hundred dollars each day.

One thing I really like about it is that I'm free. If I don't want to clean a house on Monday, maybe I'll do it Tuesday. The hours are completely flexible. I can go do things with my kids if they get a day off school. How many jobs can you do that? There's almost never anyone in the house when I'm working, so it's like having no boss, working alone at my own pace. I can laugh or sing when I work.

Most of my customers are not really wealthy, just middle class people with no time to clean their houses. Most of the houses I clean look just like mine. A lot of my clients are single men; professional men in condos who need a maid. I work for a pilot, a lawyer, a computer technician, an engineer; just single "yuppies" who don't want to clean up after themselves.

I also do some expensive houses in La Jolla. It seems like they're always more trouble. It's funny, but rich people from La Jolla or Coronado are really cheap. They want to pay you less, they never give you anything, don't like to give any bonus. Like for Christmas middle class people give me, oh, one hundred, or even two hundred dollars for a bonus but these rich people in La Jolla give me maybe ten or twenty. Or maybe they just give me Christmas presents they got before Christmas and don't even want. A box of chocolates, maybe. Rich people are tighter than other people. Most people who work for them say the same thing. They say, I guess that's how they get rich. But I don't think so. I think having too much money can change you, make you think too much of money, harden your heart.

I don't like working for rich people, but I enjoy being in fine homes with beautiful furnishings. Who wouldn't? But that's another funny thing about rich people. Some of them have such bad taste. One place I used to work the whole house was full of such cheap-looking furniture; all made out of beaten-up, unpainted boards. The floors were unpainted woods with rugs made out of rags. Everywhere there were clay pots and raw cotton cloth and iron fixtures. It looked like peasants lived there. They had crude Mexican masks on the wall, rough ceramic and paper artwork by country hicks. The *señora* always wore *ropa típica*, cotton pajamas like a refugee. What good is money if you live like that? When I told her I was buying a new table for my house in Tijuana, a nice glass table with gold legs, she acted like she was sorry for me, couldn't meet my eyes. You know where her family ate? On an old table made out of worn lumber; like something a farmer threw out fifty years ago. And their dishes were rough ceramic and the glasses were all cheap green glass with bubbles and imperfections. This is a very rich woman in a rich country! She could have gone down to Price Club and bought the very best, but the whole place looks like poor farmers live there—it's very primitive. Sometimes I feel sorry for her, paying somebody to keep that junk clean.

Another place I work now, also in La Jolla, has nice, expensive leather and silver furniture and fine polished wood. But the house is full of art. . . well, she calls it art. She says to be careful, it's very important. You should see this garbage! She has plastic boxes on the wall, with big pieces of ugly home-made paper in them. Nothing painted on the paper, maybe some stains or cuts or bird feathers or something. And there are these "sculptures" made out of junkyard metal welded together. There is a huge canvas in the living room—with no frame—that looks like somebody used it to clean tar off their paint-roller. She told me it cost over sixty thousand dollars and now is worth even more. It is pure garbage. I'm sure you could find something similar in any garbage dump.

But most of the people I work for are really close to me. They talk and tell me what's going on in their lives, I tell them about my family, my kids, just like a friendly relation-ship. I feel like if I needed help I could go to them, or they could come to me. There is no feeling of different status. Why should there be? Do you look down on a dentist because you pay him to work in your spit? Everyone does something for somebody else in order to live. That's what the economy is, what life is. The greatest among us must serve the lowest. That's from the bible, and you know it's true.

What I'm saying is, the people I work for take an inter-est in my life. Sometimes they tell me about movies I might like to see or ask me for advice. When there were those explo-sions in Guadalajara, everyone was asking me if I had any fam-ily there. Lots of them give me clothes and toys and even money for the work my church does for needy people in Tijuana and Chula Vista. They are all people I am glad to know.

There is this one old woman I've worked for seven years. She is very difficult, but I put up with all her old lady things, like an old hen in the garden. She's something else, very crabby, but I love her and take care of her and am very close to her. I feel like she's like my mother and that I'm here to take care of her. Well, it's not like she's my mother... It's that I think she needs a daughter and here I am. Not just to take care of her, they could pay a nurse for that. Of course, I'm also somebody they pay to take care of her. But it's different. I care about her and love her. I believe that the Lord brought me to her.

She was mean to me in the past, though. I used to clean for her sister, too, and she left me stuff in her will. The lady found out and lied to me, made me sign some papers. She said they were legal releases, but actually she got to keep it all, didn't give me the jewels or nothing. Or the car, an Oldsmobile worth three thousand dollars. I forgive her, though. I'm still working for her. I could have taken her to court, I guess, but I don't work like that. I believe the Lord pays everyone back.

And you know, things have changed. She's changed towards me. She used to give me nothing, she was very greedy and tight. This year she has given me over seven hundred dollars for my kids, apart from my pay. Clothes, toys, a hundred dollar Cabbage Patch Doll for my girl, a Nintendo for my boys, a cupboard, clothes for Christmas. She gives me fifty dollars for my birthday, twenty-five for my kids birthdays, sends beautiful personal cards. Some people say it's guilt, but I don't see it like that. She's a different person than she was five years ago. She's more open-handed, and more open-hearted. She laughs more, listens more, asks me about my kids. She was a miser, holding onto money and things when she was too old to use them or enjoy them. Now she's learned that things are nothing unless you give them away. My actions changed her heart. I never suffer from my way of thinking, from following the Lord's way. If you don't like religious words, call it the way of a loving heart.

You know what I should tell you? I don't know why I just thought of it, but it means something. At one house I used to clean every week, there was a little boy about seven or eight. He was a very pretty boy, but very quiet and shy, always around the house reading books instead of playing outside or watching TV. He would follow me around and try to talk to me while I was working. He used to ask me about bullfights. He was fascinated by bullfights. But I noticed he was shy about food. I would put out a tray of cookies for him every day, and a glass of milk. He would eat the cookies, but never let me see him. If I walked in and caught him eating anything he would try to hide it. He would offer me cookies, ask me if I wanted to take them home with me. Once I told him I had plenty of cookies at home, if my children hadn't swallowed them all down. He seemed surprised by that. He started asking me about my children, the things they had, the way we lived. He seemed very surprised when I'd tell him we had a television or something, got very upset when he found out my kids had no bicycles. Once he told me that if my children wanted to ride his bicycle he would loan it to them. He was a very sweet boy, but I finally understood him. He was ashamed to eat the cookie in front of me because he thought I was poor and wretched, that he was enjoying something I couldn't have. He was ashamed to be rich, in a way, because he thought I was poor. So he couldn't enjoy his cookie, the poor thing.

V. GOATISH ON AMERICA

After living in Tijuana for a little over a year I took my family back to visit Guadalajara during *Semana Santa*. My children were questioned constantly by my cousins and nephews, not about Tijuana, but about the United States. I heard my son, barely in school, tell his cousin, "You know, in the United States you never see any goats." This seemed strange to my family but after I had thought about it, I told them that it is true. In Mexico you see goats everywhere and everyone eats them. In the United States you never see goats and nobody eats them. This signifies something important about the two countries, although I am not sure what it is. In fact I am not completely sure what goats signify to me personally, but I recognize it as something on a mythical level. Goats are like cats, cocks, serpents and eagles; they serve some deep component in the subconscious, have more reality as symbols than as mere animals. So I assume there are deep meanings behind a country having or not having a population of goats.

The Bible speaks of judgment separating the sheep from the goats, as crops are separated from weeds. This seems to imply a judgment of values, and we have seen that Christianity, even Western Civilization, is often depicted as a victory over the goat. The poets refer to the Lamb of God's victory over Pan, pagan goat-foot god and lord of the goat-legged satyrs.

Throughout the background myths of the Christianization of Europe there is an image of the Good Shepherd triumphing over the cloven-hoofed enemy, the ways of pastoral fields overcoming the old wild ways of the woods. The very word "*pastor*" means "shepherd" in both Latin and Spanish. Even though I lived in the center of a large city as a girl, goats had a strong impact on my education; usually as a matter of diet, although in Mexico eating is seldom separated from other questions of grave importance.

Some of my strongest dining impressions were of goats, especially since my favorite place to eat was near our house in Sector Reforma, a small *birriaria* called La Enramada. *Birria* is a classic of the people's *cocina Mexicana*, a barbecue of goat meat on the bone in a red *chile* sauce. It is a specialty, like *pozole* or *carnitas*, and many *birriarias* offer nothing else, just three sizes of plates for three different prices. There are several different styles of *birria*, but it is known as a distinctively Jalisco dish so as I am, as we say, a "red boned" *tapatia*, I prefer the Jalisco "original recipe". *Birria* can be made of beef or other meats (sometimes very questionably when sold in tacos on the street), just as a hamburger could be made of pork or turkey or horse. But unless stated otherwise it is assumed to consist of *cabrito* or *chivito*, both words meaning "kid".

Served in a plate, with radishes and tortillas on the side, *birria* looks something like a stew, but it is cooked bones and all, often in a large, deep tray which is later tipped up to display the contents to customers. Whether out of tradition or convenience, this display of the red, dripping goat bones is common in *birriarias* and can give tourists, especially the young, a touch of the horrors. Especially since the skulls, stripped of meat but still horned and dyed a bloody red by the spices of the recipe, are usually placed on top of the heap as proof not only that the meat is actually goat, but also that the goat in question was still of a tender age.

Even to little Guadalajara girls used to the spectacle, the red tangle of massacred bones and flesh tossed in a tumble like some infernal slaughterhouse was not always a welcome sight. But we came to welcome the sight associated with good eating and good times at the back table by the whitewashed kitchen of La Enramada where we would listen to the owner and my father singing along with the three old guitarists who worked there on weekends. Our younger sisters still kept their doubts about the gruesome pile of bloody-looking body parts. One of our famous family anecdotes that always comes out on holidays or visits to restaurants with goat meat, was the time my brother "made eyes" at Cladita.

Clara was the youngest of the eight girls and was always very tender and impressionable. Even now we call her Cladita, as she called herself before she could pronounce Clarita. By the time she was four or five, she was always crying for dead animals in the streets, and having her tender sensibilities victimized by my three brothers. She never learned to watch horror movies, even to this day, and now her children tease her the way we used to. One Sunday at La Enramada, Cladita got a seat that forced her to look right at the pans of red-dripping bones and the staring, diabolic skulls on top. She got very upset and couldn't order anything to eat. Finally my brother Juan Jose volunteered to get her something else from the little *fonda* next door. I saw Juanjo stuff some radishes in his pocket as he left, but my only thoughts were on eating without getting my Sunday dress messy and maybe wondering why Juanjo would be nice to Cladita for a change. He was a typical ten year old brother, maybe a little worse.

He came back to the table carrying a plate covered with a copper pan. With a gentlemanly gesture he slid the plate in front of Cladita and whisked away the cover. When she jumped up screaming we all looked to see what Juanjo had done. He'd cut the ends off the radishes, leaving slick red balls with big white spots, then stuck the radishes in the eye sockets of the most evil-looking of the wet, red goat skulls and put in on her plate. When he lifted the copper cover, she was served with the delight of a lurid, pop-eyed vision from hell staring right back at her.

Naturally she became completely discomposed by the sight of the goat head, and started dancing up and down, shrieking. And I'm afraid the rest of us made it worse because the skull looked so comical with its cross-eyed stare. We all laughed until we were crying, especially when one of the "eyes" fell out and rolled off the table toward Clara and her collapse became complete. When Omar picked the "eye" up, toasted Cladita with it and took a big bite we were laughing so hard the red sauce was running out of our mouths and down our chins. Clara must have thought her family had suddenly turned into Satanist vampires because she ran out into the street crying for help. Even though we were all punished for torturing her so, she still reacts very ungraciously if anyone waves a pair of radishes at her, generally calling us all a pile of *cabrones*.

Mexican insults frequently involve animals; we call a stupid person *buey* or *burro*. Calling a person an ox or donkey might seem tame to Americans, who learn insults about homosexuality and perversions from urban walls, but they are strong to Mexicans because such words don't rely on the things they describe, they take on the colors of the emotions with which they are spoken. Much of Mexico is still very simple and people are still familiar with barnyard animals. It might be hard to imagine a man violating his own mother, but the behavior of goats can be observed at close hand anytime and many Spanish words formed from *chivo* or *cabra* are about insults, vice and debauchery. *Cabrón* is the standard Mexican *grosseria* or "fighting word". It means "goatish" but can't really be translated because it branches out into so many shade meanings involving cuckolding, incontinence, and all kinds of rutting and slutting around.

Whatever it is about goats that gives them that sexual reputation is probably responsible for their identification as an archetype of evil and corruption. The common image of Satan, drawn from Europe where goats were as common as they are in rural Mexico today: has the split hooves, the twisted horns, the stained beard, the pointed ears indicating a pentagonal star, the rank hair, the insinuating tail, the insatiable appetite. But the mythical goat is too capricious to remain simple: there has always been the paradoxical element of sacrifice. The image of the scapegoat is as common as the sacrificial lamb's. Which might have confused my theology, if not for my own appetite.

La Enramada will always have a traumatic nostalgia for Clara, but my own deepest impressions were of the Restaurant Nuevo Leon on Calle Independencia, a few blocks from the Merced Market and the Mariachi Plaza. As soon as I walked out of the church of San Juan del Dios, dressed in my frilly white dresses and elaborate hair ribbons, I would start sniffing the air. My father would laugh and call me a little glutton whose nose connected directly to my tummy. I'll admit I'm too fond of good food, but even at that age food meant more to me than just something to eat.

As we walked up Independencia I would start to smell the roasting goat meat and as soon as I was allowed I would run ahead to stare in the front window at a pit of coals where several young goats would be cooking in the primitive outdoor style of Nuevo Leon. Decapitated and dressed, the little bodies were leaned over the fire on wooden frames, their exposed ribcages, spread arms and bound legs making them look very much like tiny crucified humans. Staring up from the foot of the window, I saw a scene of suffering and drawn-out death that melted into my Bible study so fluidly that I still picture Golgotha as including a fire; the Savior gutted and roasting with two side orders of thief. The fusion of suffering, sacrifice, hellfire, and sacramental communion was never a mystery to me at all. It was right there on the menu.

Since there were eleven of us, my father couldn't often take us in to eat, but there were special Sundays when we could file in and sit at the high, rough tables and I could watch the cooks carve slices and joints off the little crucified scapegoats. I would eat them with my eyes closed, a private mass in which I completely felt and smelled the fruits of that long suffering; the bodies given for me, becoming part of me, and giving me life. But whenever I opened my eyes and looked up, I would be staring straight into the face of a tremendous mounted goat's head with horns spread as wide as my reach, a long white beard like a Biblical patriarch, and a gaze so obviously evil, sexual, and unclean it would have given me shivers if I hadn't seen the secrets of purification by fire, the way cooking transforms and transcends the flesh.

This discussion of bloody bones and roasting cadavers in family restaurant might seem odd to Americans, whose restaurants and markets prepare and arrange meat so that it hardly appears to have once been a living creature, but Mexican eating places frequently display the animals in their original format, dead or alive. In small restaurants in rural Jalisco, I have seen animals caged or tied in sight of the tables to be killed to order. I think this is a good thing. There is less confusion of what is happening: the Spanish word *carne* is less equivalent to the English word "meat" than to "flesh". All flesh; human as well. Flesh in the larger sense. . . the sense of carnal, of carnage, of carnival. Maybe life would be less confusing for us if we all killed our own meals.

City people think of small domestic animals as pets rather than protein factories and are unhappy with the idea of eating them. It is all a matter of what a person's palate is bred to: cooked dog would revolt most Americans, though very civilized Asians enjoy it. Farm children learn that the little animals they love and nurse to life get butchered and eaten. It is, ultimately, less a matter of good and evil than of approaching life realistically and remembering, as we try to when blessing our meals, that we live only by the grace of the moment and by absorbing the lives of other living beings. To bless food before eating it, to feel respect and responsibility for that transaction, is more naturally understood in the countryside. I think that Christianity, especially Catholicism as understood in Latin America, is more easily accepted in that context than in our modern urban lives.

But even animals with as many mystical and carnal properties as goats are also, finally, mere beasts. And as beasts, goats are so pleasant to have around that I'm surprised they aren't more popular north of the frontier. Goats are of a proper size for being around people. A mature male goat, when he stands up on hind legs to reach something else to eat, is about the same height as a young man and there is something very manlike about him; the curve of his rib cage, the way he moves. I have seen goats stand like that and had a sudden impulse to take their hooves on my shoulders and dance with them. I shared that image with my sisters and they all giggled at the picture of a herd of goats waltzing with us in our stiff dresses at cotillion lessons. You can make of my little fantasy what you wish but the reality behind it is definitely male; female goats do not resemble women at all.

Down on four legs goats are the size of dogs, comfortable and safe around the house. The kids are cute and cuddly, very sweet for pets. Goats give better milk than cows, inferior only to mother's milk as food for human babies. They clean things up, keep the grass cut, give warning of strangers approaching. And, of course, they can be eaten. The animals so famous for eating anything and everything are themselves devoured by an even more omnivorous, sexual and probably devilish species.

The odd thing is, although *birria* and other goat dishes are very characteristically Mexican, most "Mexican" restaurants in the United States don't serve goat dishes. I'm told that in American cities far from the border, serving goat is unheard of. I would invite anyone who likes Mexican food to go out of their way to try the local goat dishes. In Tijuana, of course, it is relatively easy to find good *birria*. One good place is Birriaria Guanajuanto, up in Francisco Villa. I learned of it through a listing in the restaurant guide in this newspaper and it is excellent. I prefer a place called "Guadalajara, Pues!", an extremely traditional *tapatio* type place with tile pictures of famous Guadalajara buildings and pictures of the owner's career with the Guadalajara *futbol* team, the Chivas. This is one place you can see the piles of bones and huge stuffed goat heads but unfortunately its location at 158 Constitución (at the bottom of the hill, between First and Cuahuila) is in a very seedy part of town. Family groups might be offended by the drunkenness and prostitution that surrounds the restaurant in the evenings, although the goats grinning on the wall seem to approve.

There are also some *birriarias* on the American side of the border, especially in Chula Vista. Birriaria Sinaloa, in the shopping center at Broadway and Main comes richly recommended, even by such a delicate *tapatia* as my sister Clara. (They keep the skulls in the kitchen.)

Other styles of goat meat can be found in Tijuana, but the most convenient and one of the best is Las Brasas restaurant at Ninth and Madero, one block east and south of the Jai Alai fronton. The specialty is cowboy cooking in the style of the Sinaloa and Monterrey ranges. They serve *birria estilo de Jalisco* and barbecue of lamb as well as several traditional dishes of goat meat, including the Nuevo Leon *a las brasas* style with a whole kid skewered over open coals and *cabrito al pastor*, cooked "shepherd style" by rotating over open flames.

And we arrive again at sheep and goats. A friend once mentioned to me an American book called "A Nation of Sheep." I never read the book, but I remembered that image as I started to investigate the United States. Is this the famous "American dream"; a woolly, sheepish life of herds that are protected to be sheared? It is the dream of English landscape paintings and I think I can see it from the hills above Chula Vista, or from the cross on top of Mount Soledad; regular squares of peace, fields of grass cut very short and neat, dogs to protect against the wolves. The order and peace and cleanliness in this country is a very pretty vision, especially to people from Tijuana where things are rough, disordered, unsafe and ugly. If you travel into the *barrancas*, the communities piled up the canyons, you will start up steep, narrow dirt paths through trash piles and rocky confusion. You will walk into a rough male world of violence, drinking, salvaging and harsh treatment. And you will start to see goats running in the paths, eating the trash, playing in the rubble. You can just drive across the border, park your car and walk up into Goatland. But to go the other direction to the organized, clean, trusting fields of Sheepland, is a much more difficult trip which can take forever and cost everything you have. As a guide in either direction I can only advise an awareness of diet and what eating really means to both the eater and the eaten.

VI. GAMES OF HAZARD

STREET GAMES

The streets north of Tijuana's Avenida Juarez are not the kind of neighborhood for people like me. So when I have reason to walk there, I always learn things. Some of the things are funny or horrible. Sometimes they are magic.

There was a big knot of people between the buses and buildings on First Avenue and to pass I would have had to brush against some very dirty and probably touchy people, so I walked out into the street. I was almost around the crowd when I saw they were watching some sort of game. A handsome *muchacho* in his twenties, wearing the typical black narco-cowboy clothes, was moving three aluminum bottle caps back and forth on a cardboard poster laid on top of a garbage can. I stood behind him, watching him move the caps, and saw a dried green pea rolling under the caps as he swished them around. We used to call the game, "Where's Granny?"

The caps tilted away from him a little and I was sure that I, standing out in the street away from the action, was the only one who could see the pea. If I'd been taller, I'm sure I wouldn't have noticed it. I very clearly saw the pea under the cap to my right when he stopped and asked for bets. Another young fellow with a lot of assurance held up ten thousand pesos to the *muchacho*, but he made a sour face and everyone

113

laughed. Twenty thousand, then. Well, OK; where is she? The bettor smiled like a winner and touched the middle cap. I smiled and shook my head and, thinking the game was over, pointed to the cap on the right. The *muchacho* kept his hands away from the board, told the betting man to take a look. No pea under the middle cap. Sorry, amigo. . . but what's twenty thousand worth these days, anyway?

But two men in their forties with very expensive clothes and briefcases were taking an interest. One of them, who had been looking directly at me when I pointed to the cap on the right, reached out to tip that cap over. Wait a minute, wait a minute; if the *señor* is interested, he needs to make it interesting. The man laughed and reached into his pockets. His friend was excited, telling him what a good chance it was with the odds reduced to only one against one; but the man couldn't find any money. This kind of man writes checks and uses Banamex VISA. The crowd was waiting, suspecting him of making excuses. His friend offered a few thousand pesos from his own pocket. No, wait. The man was now totally committed, a professional executive whose decision had been made. He pulled out his wallet, an accordion of plastic cards. The *muchacho* said sorry, but he really wasn't in a position to accept "American Express" and the crowd laughed at the way he pronounced the English words. The briefcase man pulled a folded bill from behind one of the cards and unfolded it. The bill was one hundred dollars, more than a quarter of a million of pesos. That shut the crowd up.

The *muchacho* waved the man off: he couldn't possibly let the man lose such a large sum. The man insisted and the crowd started shifting to his side. Now who is making excuses? Embarrassing for the *muchacho*, who had to admit he couldn't match the wager. The crowd laughed at him. The executive sensed his victory and was gracious about it: he would wager his bill against whatever the *muchacho* had in his pocket. And his belt. It was a nice enough belt, with an intricate turquoise buckle, but mostly he wanted to see the younger man have to strip the belt off in public, have to hold his pants up with his hands. A sly piece of macho symbolism that the crowd appreciated at once. The younger man looked down at his belt, shrugged, and motioned at the bottle caps, which had been sitting untouched, gathering mystique. The executive was relaxed and cheerful as he reached out and turned the right hand cap over empty. He didn't even glance when the *muchacho* tipped the left hand cap to show the pea—he just stared at the place where there was no pea.

The *muchacho* took the hundred dollars almost apologetically and praised the older man for being a sportsman and for having some massive *cojones*. Just not such good luck. Anyone else want a try? The man who only lost twenty thousand said it was too much for him and the crowd seemed to agree, moving away from the game. The twenty-thousand-peso loser started talking to the hundred-dollar man, asking how it was possible that between them they had failed. The executive just shook his head, but the conversation around him got very excited. I watched the executive, trying to see it he would look at me, if he was so convinced because of the movement I had made. I myself was completely stunned. I SAW the pea there. The man's loss was impossible. I looked at the board again for some explanation, but the bottle cap cowboy was gone.

As you might expect, I didn't forget about that little game in the street. I had been amazed, had felt guilty, felt like a fool. But mostly it was the curiosity and wonder about how things happen that has eaten at my mind since I was a schoolgirl. I was doomed from an early age to write for newspapers.

The man with the briefcase may have had more credit, but I have better luck. Two weeks later I was taking a bus to the *linea* and saw the *muchacho* from the bottle cap game get on the bus with another young man who I later recognized as the small loser from the pea game. They looked around, taking everyone's measurement. I don't know if we looked too smart for games or too stupid to know much about music, because they started singing. They did a sentimental old *ranchero* tune a little too experienced to sound right from boys their age, one singing a harmony slightly delayed behind the other. They were truly terrible. But they still collected a few coins and smiles from other passengers. I pulled out my purse and looked around inside it while the bus emptied, then told the *muchachos* I would buy them a drink, or several drinks in the Scorpion Bar if they would talk with me awhile. They didn't look at each other before saying yes. I'm sure they assumed I was a lonely housewife in search of a youth movement. Mexican men can be counted to draw such conclusions.

They had several sips of expensive tequila before I told them I'd seen their game downtown and wanted to know more. The second youngster looked startled but the bottle cap artist just winked at me and made the noted pincer sign with his finger and thumb. I wouldn't have to pay them too much. They were on their way out of town. They mentioned recent talks with the police, conversations in which money also changed hands but which they'd found less enjoyable. They have a poor opinion of the local law, an assessment which is apparently mutual.

They gave their names as "Pancho" and "Paco", which might even have been true, but they call themselves "Los Allala", a name that could be interpreted at several devious or risqué levels. Shockingly, they think of themselves primarily as a musical group. It appears that the group varies in size, always including my informants but sometimes having as many as eight members. Other than future musical stardom, the purpose of the group is, as they put it, *desplumar pichones*—plucking the feathers of "pigeons". The hundred dollar performance I saw was one of their repertoire pieces called *la corchalata*, but they knew other classic tunes and were capable of spontaneous improvisation.

116

"You are surprised I wasn't working alone?" Pancho smiled at me, shaking his head as though our ages were reversed. "You still don't know that there were three others working with us that day. When you approach a game like that on the streets you should assume that you are the only one not on the payroll, see? The whole thing will be for your benefit. Like a troupe of actors, you see? You come in, you pay, you are entertained. The more fun you have, the more you pay. It's very fair and progressive, the *corchalata*."

The day I saw the group "perform", there were four *riatas*, or "lariats" roping pigeons in to Pancho, the *uña*, or "claw" who moved the caps around. "It's mostly a matter of making men feel that their macho demands that they play the manly game," Pancho said. The *riatas* are just trying to make that happen. Everyone, even the man who spits and walks off cursing the *uña*, is actually playing against the *pichón* whose money we are trying to earn."

Even me, I said. Paco laughed, saying, "Yes. You were beautiful pointing to the cap like that." Had they let me see the pea on purpose? "You and a couple of other people. Though most react only with their eyes."

But the man with the hundred-dollar bill wasn't part of the troupe? "Fortunately not. But we'd have to say he played his part magnificently, no?" Paco laughed again, "Much better than we normally expect from amateurs. We could use more volunteers of his capacity."

But I very definitely saw the pea under the right-hand cap and Pancho never touched it again. How did it get under the other cup? Both boys smiled at me like adults with a secret from a child. Pancho said, "Well, that is our real trade, see"? We had to apprentice ourselves to learn it and it wouldn't be fair to our "union" to pass it on. At least not for so little money. But I can tell you this much. . . "He spread his hands and looked up as if watching something fly out of his palms". "It's magic."

I hadn't expected any lessons, so I wasn't disappointed. The *muchachos* raised their glasses to drink to my health and when I tapped my own glass against theirs I suddenly noticed a dried pea floating in it. They laughed at my face and I bought them more drinks. The pea in my glass was, of course, impossible. Or maybe the waiter was part of their scheme. Or perhaps the tequila bottler? I have kept the pea to serve me as a lesson in the uses of magic and credulity.

But Los Allala have other talents. They have done a little bit of everything, depending upon their numbers resources, and opportunities. "Last year we did very well passing counterfeit American twenty-dollar bills, especially down south in tourist places. It was a great idea that worked until too many people came in and everybody was alerted. See, an American twenty is a pretty big bill—over sixty thousand pesos—but very common for Americans; they pass them out all the time. They're as easy to print here as up there, but our edge is that Mexicans are less familiar with them, haven't handled them all their lives, you see?

"The first ones we had were great, the best *falso* I've ever seen. I heard an old guy in Mazatalan was making it, using bleached thousand peso notes. A cheap way to get the good paper, see. And, to Mexicans, they had the feel of a peso bill. We put them in the pockets of old Levi's and ran them through a washing machine until they felt and looked old. They were perfect.

"We were paying just under twelve thousand *barros* for pieces of paper worth over sixty thousand, so we were making almost fifteen dollars per "bite". But then a flood of cheap *falso* came in and made everybody start looking close at the twenties and the odds went down. Then we couldn't even get the good stuff anymore. That's Mexico for you—it's like a guy puts up a *palapa* selling shrimp and beer on a little beach somewhere, next time there's ten, twenty, a *chingo* of them and nobody's making a living at it. It's a shame, but that's how this business is. Things that work too well, they go out of circulation for awhile. But if you listen to the old guys they'll tell you everything comes back sooner or later."

Los Allala learned what they call the "soft-change game" in Los Angeles; they give a fairly large bill like an American ten or Mexican fifty thousand for merchandise worth a dollar or two, then change their minds and start a confusing series of changes which leaves the seller with less money than he had before he sold to them. The game is harder to play in Mexico where money is dearer and eyes are sharper. But still, there are times. . . .

"That's what we're looking for, not the right plan or location. We're looking for the right person at the right time. The little girl whose father stepped out for a beer and left her in charge, the record store clerk flirting with a pretty girl and wanting to look quick and casual. We just walk around the streets looking for chances."

And it is a chance.

"You are taking chances every time you do something like that. Sometimes the drooling, half-blind old fool at the *fonda* turns out to be a sharp old goat after all. Or the little girl watching her mama's stand is some sort of arithmetic genius and calls her two-meter cousin over to straighten things out. Once we tried to sell the old 'ticket to Los Angeles' to a policeman's wife who was just at the bus station waiting for her sister to come in. Maybe we can play stupid and talk our way out. Maybe we have to run for it. It's a gamble every time we open up our shop. So you see? We are gamblers after all. We're risking our *nachas* out here. Funny thing, though. When we're just doing our normal business, we're taking risks, but when we're running games of chance, there's no risk involved at all. It's the oldest joke in the show. The pigeon says, 'I don't play games of chance'. And we say, 'Yeah, brother, neither do we'."

DEATH GAMES

I went to the *palenque* to hear Ana Gabriel sing, not to see roosters tear each other apart. But the roosters came before Srta. Gabriel. I am by no means a follower of rooster fights. Less from humanity, I think, than from boredom. Nevertheless, the *palenque* is an important Mexican cultural event, with the ambiance, history and behavior of the others attending more interesting than what occurs in the fighting pit. I think it is indispensable in understanding the behavior of Mexican men. The behavior of Mexican women is completely beyond my comprehension.

Palenque used to be a village event, a tournament of fighting cocks with auxiliary events like music, dancing, feasting, drunkenness, and fighting. The combination of competition with other ranches and towns, heavy betting, family feuds, and a *macho* party attitude could usually be counted on to produce injuries, pregnancies, and other personal disasters. In the *corridos,* like the *Corrido del Gallero* as sung by Vincente Fernandez, the hero rides in on his wonderful horse with his beautiful *gallo,* wins all the money, shoots anyone who objects, and rides off with the blushing *chinaca* behind him on the saddle.

It took me most of my life to realize that the behavior of humans at *palenque* is influenced by the behavior of the gorgeous birds that are the stars of the show. They are the emphatically beautiful, the strutting perfection of animal masculinity, genetically pre-ordained to impregnate any female and kill any male that their eye should fall on. The men, especially after a bottle of Tequila or Mezcal, are impressed by this display and emulate it in the way men everywhere emulate their sports heroes.

The only female models in this most male of diversions are the singers, who come into the ring later, when cloths have been thrown over the splatters of blood. They dress like sexy sirens or cowgirls in a ring of male musicians: delicate, protected flowers. Though they might step to the side of the ring to receive flowers or an adoring kiss of the hand from male admirers. In the days before television the colorful, violent *palenque* traditions were a core of local life and inspired many songs and paintings, in addition to life styles.

Today, in Tijuana, it is a quieter affair. The men dress as usual, there are no horses tied outside for getaways or spontaneous racing. The musicians play electric instruments, the people sit on permanent cement seats. The night I saw Ana Gabriel there were only three fights among men in the seats; but only with fists, not knives or guns.

The brave roosters attack each other each time they are fronted and released, sometimes in fierce, slashing aerial acrobatics, other times merely staggering towards each other until one is too dead to respond and the other is the "winner". But still the men watch the way the cocks inflate into furious balls of bright feathers, the way they keep returning to the fight even when they are trailing blood, the way they will risk dying over the chance to continue the line of their seed. The men are very interested in all of this, and in which cock will win. The air is full of flying green tennis balls as bets are placed, each ball slit to hold bet receipts as boys throw them into the crowd and money as they are thrown back. As the big balls of large bills fly around, the men watch their champions perform.

Maybe it was my thoughts about fighting cocks as role models, but I was very shocked to see one of the *galleros* give his cock several injections just seconds before placing him in the ring. My curiosity led me to explanations from a man who admits that cocks are the most significant thing in his life. He explains, at least, the part about the injections.

"That's a unique thing about *gallos*—it's not like horse racing, or the Olympics, where you get in trouble for doping. You can give the birds whatever drugs you think they need. They sell all these pills to thicken the blood so there won't be easy bleeding or internal hemorrhage; everything from Vitamin K to defatted liver hemoglobin cells. There are analgesics—they claim 'non-narcotic', right?—to add "bottom" to a bird, make him more game.

"You can get electrolytes, caffeine compounds, all those central nervous system stimulants. They're mostly based on *nux vomica*, which is actually strychnine. You can get testosterone capsules, steroids to build their muscles during the keep. You can give them amphetamines and cocaine if you want. I've seen people shoot a mixture of cocaine and heroin into a bird. They even advertise this 'Hot Shot' that comes in time-release pills or ampules for last-minute injections. Their logo says, 'No Bleed, No Die, Just Fight, Fight, Fight.' It's supposed to create a killing frenzy that actually allows the bird to kick and fight beyond normal death. Well. . . I don't know. Everyone knows a bird can run and fly with his head cut off, but I don't believe a dead bird can still fight. It might make a good movie for Steven King."

But he doesn't believe in using such drugs on his own birds.

"Except Vitamin K against bleeding. I could say it's philosophical; I don't like the idea of having a bunch of *drogadictos* in my stable. But the truth is, I don't think those things work. I know a guy who really believes in steroids. His birds get these big strong breasts and legs, there's no doubt. And they win a lot. But they also lose a lot. The steroids make them demented, they have no concentration, no game. It damages their *macho*, their maleness. So if his kind of *pollo loco* could always beat my birds, I guess I'd have to try his methods. But they don't. And for every *gallero* out there using a whole drug store on his cocks, there's some country boy saying the reason his bird has just won twenty-two straight fights is because he keeps them on natural grass pasture with such and such seed and fertilizer and so many goats to fertilize and keep the grasshoppers stirred up so the cocks can kill and eat them.

"Also, to me, there's this question. Understand, to me the pride is in producing these birds, creating winners. When my bird wins, it's like. . . like my painting got a prize. My wife says I play God with my cocks, and in a way I do. I love these birds and I can't imagine giving them strychnine or cocaine. But what if I had to, to keep them alive? What if it worked? Would those wins breed true? No. You'd end up with chickens that can't win without drugs. My birds breed true. I breed for a smart, agile, game bird—that's what I admire. And every bird, every fight, every little wing beat or flick of the feet in every fight is a characteristic of that bird's lineage. Those drug store cockers cheat the future generations. I don't."

What techniques does he use, if not chemicals?

"First of all, you choose the breeding stock to produce the best birds. You look at other cocks and hens, judging their qualities. You look for certain obvious signs. A big hen with a strong tail that will support them if they are pushed back on it. If they put their feet down, they're doomed. And a deep, strong breast, a good neck. The wings are the most important because they fly into each other. They could have bad legs and still win if they have the power in their wings.

"But beyond that there are things I look at that I couldn't explain. Like feather color. I'm looking at a certain Kelso cross and maybe comparing the color to other crosses I've seen. These are not unrelated characteristics, they strong tail is important for guiding the attack flight and also for support. All part of the genetic package. The deadliness and beauty come together.

"All my birds are *giros*, a three-quarter cross from Red Fox Grey stock, bloodlines pioneered by Oscar Akins and Johnny Jumper. I find them the most beautiful of birds, and I believe they are the winningest, the very best fighters with one inch blades. Every other *giro* I ever see, I'm looking at it, comparing my birds to it. If I see something I want, I might buy a stud from that farm. I recently paid eight hundred dollars for

123

a pure Grey rooster, just to get his seed for the future. I see hundreds of Greys and would recognize them again in a minute, though to most people they look the same. As my wife says, 'They'd all look the same to Colonel Sanders.' And a lot of guys would argue with this—and sometimes when you talk to cockers you'd think you were in a genetics class at the University—but hens are more important than the roosters in producing good fighters. Especially when you're breeding for bottom. The game streak comes from the hens.

"You find other cockers who are just as committed to Roundhead cocks, or Hatch or Leiper or Blueface. That Lieper/Blue is not a bad cross. You have to cross: pure strains are not the best fighters. So you cross and hope to get something better. When you find a good mixture, you breed brother to sister, trying to isolate the good traits. This always produces the best animals. It also produces the worst animals, but you just discard those and work with the good ones.

"When I say 'the best' birds, you understand that I'm talking about the best for a certain type of fight. Mostly, for a certain kind of weapon. The Hawaiian tradition is almost completely an aerial show, one big jump to death. In Asia they use very long knives. The Filipino weapon is two and a half inches long. So you want a very fast, agile bird. In the United States, they use gaffs, a round, pointed spike like a nail. There is a lot of beating with the sides of the gaff and you hear gringo cockers talking about how to control internal bleeding. In Mexico we mostly use the one inch *navaja*, curved like a saber and sharpened on the inside of the curve. This requires a much gamer bird than the Asian fighting. By game I mean a bird with bottom, that will hang in there, take wounds and keep fighting, survive out of sheer will to dominate. A bird with endurance and guts. Now Cuban fighting is with the bird's natural spurs. It's very hard for them to kill, a fight can last for hours. So you see these big, strong birds like Blue Cubans, or Toppies; birds of Spanish Jerezano bloodlines.

"If you think about it, what would be the 'best' human body type for fighting? Obviously for fist-fighting you'd want a big, strong Mike Tyson type of individual. But if the fight is with straight razors where one touch could mean death, you'd want a very fast individual with long arms and quick hands. A Bruce Lee type, or better yet Michael Jordan. The best body is the one that suits the weapon. I'll tell you, boxing would have a different mystique if the loser died. Or if we could breed fighters.

"Speaking of fighting with a naked heel, those are the most brutal, bloody fights. But that is the natural mode. People think it's so cruel and barbaric to strap knives on these birds and let them fight to the death. But that's their natural way, their genetic programming. We breed and feed and train them—give them a better chance, make them better fighters, with better seed. And we give them steel *navajas* to fight with, better than the spurs they are born with. They will fight to the death anyway. With the *navajas* it's less painful, more humane. Would you rather be stabbed to death or beaten to death? With a steel weapon a bird can sometimes kill his enemy instantly with a clean cut on the very first jump. Is that so brutal? They are just chickens, you know.

After choosing, breeding, and feeding the birds, there is the matter of conditioning.

"The result comes down to the keep. It's the final conditioning period before a fight, an isolation and intense training to bring the bird to its lowest weight and a peak of stamina, speed and endurance. Just like any athletic training, really. A keep can be anything from three to twenty days and you can buy all these courses and programs on how to do it—what exercises, what food, how much water, periods of rest, periods of light and darkness. They're like "Charles Atlas" books for birds. Except the birds don't need will power. I do a lot of jumping with my birds, to build the wings. You pick them up at the tail a certain way and they have to flap their wings or they'll fall over on their face. They have no choice but to get stronger.

"Meanwhile, I'm giving them a feeding I've developed over years. Some people will be giving them steroids during the keep, vitamins, all sorts of things. I play a radio really loud while I'm training them, really obnoxious stations, to get them used to noise. Otherwise, they might be distracted in the pit with all those people yelling. The keep is a very intense, intimate period with the birds and by the end of it they're at their fighting perfection. To me it's the most enjoyable part of bringing them from an egg to a victor. My methods are totally individual, most winning cockers have their unique methods. And there are some who say the best training for winning fighters is 'incubator conditioning'. That is to say, giving a bird the best parents.

"I used to do everything, including handling the birds in the pit. But when you're fighting thousand-dollar birds for big money, you specialize more. I work with two other fighters, who are good at the *palenque* but bored by breeding. Alberto, we call him "Cacho", is our *amárador*; he does the heeling, putting the weapons in place. Which is a pretty important job since it all comes down, finally, to the point of the spike. I let him saw the spurs off their legs in the first place, so the stump will be just like he wants it. Before the fight he covers the stump with a little sock, the *botana*, or with moleskin. Then he chooses just the right weapon. He has a big collection of *navajas* and you'd be surprised what those little knives cost. I've seen him pay ninety dollars apiece for some Filipino weapons. I have some fifty-dollar bayonets myself. The length of the weapon is limited by the rules of the fight, of course. But he picks a weight and curvature he thinks best for the particular cock. The cocks strike with an oval motion, both legs rotate across and cross at the ankle. But each one has a little different motion and you want the point coming straight in. If there is not enough curve, the point might hit the ground, too much and he will be striking with the back of the blade. You can't train the motion, it's instinctive, one of the qualities you breed for. So you choose the right tool. Cacho has good eyes for these things, differences of millimeters in a motion almost too fast to be seen.

"So he fits the socket of the weapon over the *botana*, then ties it on with special string made just for that purpose. Strong, flat, light like dental floss. Like lacing the gloves on a boxer. He has good hands for it, always gets it on perfect. You can't exaggerate the importance of a bird being well-heeled. Then he puts a sheath over the *navaja* for protection and turns him over to Chuy, the *esoltador*.

"Chuy is another specialist, he handles the bird and lets him loose. Part of what he does is the feeling the birds get in his hands. Nothing I could explain, but he sends signals to the bird just in the way he touches him he signals. . . I don't know, calm, confidence, a sort of aura. If that sounds too spiritual for you, you should realize that almost everything the birds do from the first displays to the final death is a complicated set of signals to each other. Chuy sends the same signals to the cock that the bird itself is sending: it's already over, that other *pollo* is already roasting in the *molé*. When he steps up to the line, Chuy is watching the other bird, the other *esoltador*, looking for anything false, anything he doesn't like, maybe just suddenly realizing that we can't win it. He can quit the fight any time, up until the *árbitro* takes the sheath off the *navaja* and wipes it with lime juice to make sure it's clean and not poisoned. Then the birds are crossed and there is no backing down.

"Chuy holds the bird just so, for the best release, its legs held up in the right "V" position for the initial attack. And he releases it with just the right touch, the right timing. And he's got to be ready to grab the bird the second he hears the command to handle. Too quick you're disqualified, too late, maybe your bird is dead from a lucky shot. Before the birds are faced the second time, Chuy can nurse the bird a little. A lot of it is just his hands, but he knows everything to do to combat shock, bring a bird back into the spirit. You can't use any medicine or anything on the bird during the fight, not even chalk for bleeding, only hands and breath. For instance, if the bird is losing blood or experiencing shock, his crest will start to pale, a bad sign and possibly one that will be interpreted by the other bird. But it is permitted for the handler to blow or suck on the comb, pulling blood into it. This does much to bring a cock around into fighting spirit. On the other hand, it is prohibited to place a finger in the bird's vent and stimulate his testicles. Somebody decided a long time ago how much of this strange intimate behavior with fowls is fair to use in a fight.

"If there is no win in the second facing, the birds are moved in and placed at the short range marks, *las cortas*, the final period. This is where a good handler can win a fight. By now both birds will be bleeding, shocked and close to death. And at the *cortas* the birds are not released, just placed on the ground. You have to hold them by the feathers on their backs and set them down, then let them go. Sometimes one or both birds will just sit there, sometimes they are already dead when they are released. There is a rule about birds falling over dead; the bird whose beak touches the ground first loses. So it sometimes happens that a dead bird, if the handler has placed it just right, might stay erect, while a live bird tries to attack, then falls over and loses. So you see? A dead bird can win a fight after all. If he does, give credit to the *esoltador*.

There is obviously a lot of love for these birds, but it can't be denied that the betting is very important.

"Of course not. Most of the people know nothing about cocks. The betting is the thing, and the money is very serious. At the Californias Fair tournament you pay a deposit of twenty thousand pesos just to get in. Twenty million pesos minimum first prize. Seven thousand dollars. American tournaments have fifty-thousand-dollar purses, in the Filipinas you see prizes of one hundred twenty thousand dollars, single bets of eighteen thousand. And that's where the real money is, the bets. You don't just walk in and put down the money. You have to have *prestígio,* a record. You have to be a contender. The way it works is that each fight has a favorite, either from the red side of the ring or the green side. The other bird is wagered at a handicap. So at eighty percent you can bet eight dollars against the favorite and win ten. Or bet ten on the favorite and only win eight. The lowest discount is seventy percent. Less a match than that would be ridiculous. So an inferior bird doesn't get into the real fights. Some cockers just buy their way in, but nobody respects it. Like people know when a boxer is fighting some punk who shouldn't even be in the same ring.

"It's not a game where you think about luck, but there's luck involved. Some nights the favorites win every fight, sometimes none. Maybe you have a really great bird against some loser that is laid off at seventy percent, but in the first attack your bird just sticks his breast right onto the *navaja* by pure fluke. What can you do then? Pick up your bird and pay off, that's all. No matter that you've thought of everything.

"But is life so different? Listen what happened to me, to us, last fall. You know fighting cocks is legal in Mexico, but it's illegal to bet on them, which comes to the same thing. People think of this as a Mexican sport, but it's actually illegal here. It's biggest in the United States, completely legal in Arizona, Texas, Georgia, Ohio, Kansas, Hawaii, Louisiana, Alabama, Arkansas. Isn't their president from Arkansas, and a chicken man himself? All of the gear for fighting comes from *norteamericano* suppliers; the cages, the feed, the drugs, the scorekeeping software, the videos on genetics and sparring and heeling and training and dominant selection. But here in Mexico *palenque* is actually against the law. No problem, you pay off the law. Or you "prestige" them off. I'm sure you know that ninety percent of the big bettors are mafiosos and drug traffickers. Who else has that kind of money? You see a man bet ten thousand dollars on a single fight, at eighty-five percent against the favorite no less, and you know he didn't get the money selling *carne asada*.

"So the *mordida* is in, everything is okay and everyone is happy; the Mexican way. The pit at La Gloria pays off the *judiciales* in one district, the Florido pit pays off their own '*judas*'. Every detail attended to. But in November President Carlitos comes to town and brings a bunch of capital city *federales* with him. These guys have no 'turf', no loyalty, no payoff, no respect. They just gobble up everything they see. So they raid the *palenque* at la Gloria. Grab everybody there and take us to jail. They confiscate all my betting money, my birds, my equipment—probably over two thousand dollars worth— then they set me a fifteen hundred dollar bail and are thinking over how much they are going to fine me. And they put me on six months probation that I can't risk going to a fight. And they shut down the La Gloria pit. They arrested two hundred people, but when the story went out in the newspaper there were twenty-five names listed. Mine, of course, but nobody from 'Chapu' who drives a Cherokee and wears thousand- dollar boots, right? Those rich mafioso bastards probably even got their money back. But you see what I mean? You can plan everything, pay the toll, work hard. . . and still you get the *chingada*.

"I'll get the money and get back into the game. Money is not everything here. What's important to me is that my birds can compete against anyone, that I have personally bred winning fighters, watch them fight to prove their blood, do all I can to improve that blood. It doesn't matter to me if a cock of mine wins or loses as long as he fights game. If he runs or loses in some ridiculous way, I can't stand that. But if he fights a good fight, I'll be proud of him win or lose.

"There's an old joke that people aren't as smart as cocks because cocks never bet on people. But don't they? Aren't they really betting their lives that I've done them right? I'm more than their trainer; I'm like God to them. I chose who their parents would be, what they would be like. I feed them what I want and make them do all these strange things. I make decisions that will make them live or die. And they don't even know it. They probably think I'm just a pair of hands."

After you listen to enough of these hymns about cockfighting, you realize they are all, above all, romances. Romance between a man and his bird. If I had used the word "cock" in that sentence, it would have had a second sense in English. But in Mexico the word "bird" has the same significance, the phallus. Quite probably such expressions arise in the subconscious.

The point is, the relationship between *gallo* and *gallero* is an intimate one beyond the usual scope of sport; it is a relationship of affection, pride, possession—a living, a bond to the death. Men who hardly speak to their wives spend hours stroking, grooming and crooning to their roosters. All towards that moment when they release them into the flying knives of another man's little beauty. To win is more than having thrown a ball or horseshoe correctly, to lose is far more than watching dice roll to an unfortunate number. The art of *palenque* always shows two birds in full display clashing in spectacular viciousness. What I commemorate as a touching and vulnerable moment, is a man kneeling just before releasing his bird, holding his hopes and feelings in his hand like a clump of beautiful, fragile feathers and trying, as no lover ever has done, to project his will past the barriers of flesh, and live for a brief, bloody instant in the gleaming eye of a being he loves to the death.

LIFE GAMES

"You're right," the man sitting in the club seating at the Jai Alai Book told me, "Those guys are in love with those birds. They act like they're women or heroic champions, but they're just chickens after all; beautiful, but brainless as cabbages. Lots of those guys love their roosters more than their wives. Like that Vincent Fernandez record, 'Today I'm Talking To My Cock.' Well, I don't find chickens so good for conversation, myself. Those guys. . . well, probably they loved their wives when they first knew them. When they were girls. Beautiful and brainless. Actually, I bet on cocks myself. But a business relationship, not mooning over some damned rooster."

He's a man of average size and looks, and was obviously very much at home in the jai alai *fronton* and the betting book next door. His clothing is very *flamante*, a cobalt silk shirt and daringly pleated carbon pants; clothes that look fast and disreputable on a man in his forties. He has an eye for fashions, and discussed my dress and scarf before telling me where he bought everything he was wearing. He shops sales at Dorians and loves to go by the Broadway's shop for young men.

"I can see what you're thinking. The cheap, superficial gambler with fancy clothes he can't really afford. Am I right?" Well maybe I did have some thoughts like that.

"You know who I am, then. Flashy, cheap, superficial, temporary. I'm a hippodrome whore. But I know who you are, too. Just by looking at your clothes, hearing your questions. I'm what you want for your story, am I right? So you're after a little cheap excitement from the dark edges of life to shock your conservative readers. Am I right?"

Well yes, here I am.

"But what if I tell you that I'm a working man, an ordinary person with a family, doing the best I know to keep my life on its legs? What if I told you that gaming is a big industry in Tijuana and always has been? Or that it's a major part of the local economy and society? Would that make it all too boring for you, would it?"

We should find out, don't you think?

"What do you think of the jai alai? I nice piece of brick, am I right? And you've seen the hippodrome? The park, the zoo, the statues, the nice building? It used to be even nicer, like stepping out of a garbage pile into a dream. You realize it's one of the oldest buildings in town, you realize? There were races and games and big casinos here a long time before there were factories and paved streets, believe me.

"You see, I'm the rarest bird, a native of Tijuana. One hundred percent *cachanilla* like we say. I can remember before all the *glorietas* and glass buildings and chromium, I can remember. Back when "Tia Juana" was just a filthy, dusty, crazy little piggery. And a lot more fun to live in.

"My father was a gambler too, back when Tijuana had some of the finest casinos anywhere. When the Caliente Casino had a solid gold salon and big Hollywood stars came here to play. My pop would play up with any of them, my pop would. He'd come home one night with the biggest bottle of Ollitas Reposada, handing out twenty centavo coins to every kid in the barrio. Then another night he might lose everything but his underpants and my mother would have to go ask my cousins for food and be forced to listen to long sermons about the evils of gambling, men in general, and one dissolute evil man in particular detail. My mother was always either suffering like a martyred *santa* or being treated like a queen married to a mafioso. But she never said a word against my father or his ways. She loved him, you see. And she was in it for the thin years and the fat ones—she'd put her money down on that man and didn't back off. She was the only woman in the family who didn't 'toss the corner' when it was obvious that I was going to become a gambler myself. My own wife is the same way; she never complains. But the rest of her family does. Apparently they constantly find me less than responsible. They ask if this gives me shame. I tell them it does, but I somehow find the strength to bear it.

"What they don't understand is that money itself means nothing to me. I mean money like this here on the table. What is it but a symbol? It means only what we want it to mean. When I'm gambling, I'm not thinking, '¡*Hijole*! I could win a million pesos, think of what that would buy me.' Any more than, I don't know, a chess player would care about what he might get for selling the bishop he just captured. You see? Money is for scoring the big game, and also my power to perform, and my "ranking" in the game. If there was a world championship, like boxing or something, it would be decided by how much money. So if people look at me and say, 'That *cabrón* is playing with money his family needs for food and shoes and school books,' they don't see the point. From my view, those things are irrelevant drains on my game, on my power and status, my living. The very food I eat comes out of my *taco*, the roll of cash that lets me play and to win money. Can you understand that?

"Sometimes, when my luck has been bad, I feel ashamed to be saving up money while my wife and children need things. But that's not because I'm gambling, it's because I'm losing, because times are hard. Would you criticize a *taxista* who can't pay for birthday parties and school books because he needs the money to fix up the taxi that earns the money in the first place? What is the difference? Furthermore, I suspect that if I were a fireman or a cop or a politician, my in-laws would still complain that I'm doing my wife wrong, risking my life and her daily bread. I think there is very little any man can do to keep from those kind of family pressures and emotions, so why worry about it? The best thing I can do for my family is keep winning.

"Then of course a man has to eat—if I lose at tennis it would embarrass me, if I lose here at the *fronton* I don't have anything to eat. But players are a close class of people, in some ways like an order or a brotherhood. We have our traditions and take care of each other, even though we compete with each other. For instance, if I needed money to pay for food or rent, I could come in here and just let people know it. I wouldn't have to ask anybody, maybe just the way I'm sitting and not playing would let them know without my opening my mouth. Somebody would ask me if I needed a little money until my horses get smarter. These are generous men, and at any time somebody in the game is winning, just as somebody is always losing. I myself would not hesitate to loan any of these guys a few hundred dollars with no questions, never mention when it should be paid back. Because who knows when? That's a pretty basic reality around here—Who knows? After all, that's what makes gambling possible.

"Loans like that are a sort of security system for guys like us, guys with no more security than the next roll of the dice or the next *cretino* missing an easy kill shot. But such a loan would be for personal welfare, not for playing. Absolutely not. If I borrow money to live on, I'd better not be seen playing here until I've paid it back. Or anywhere, actually; there is almost no place in this town I could play any kind of game without my colleagues knowing about it. And how I did. You don't joke around with these things, either, or you lose your *protége* in this community. If it's a lot of money, you might lose more than that. If somebody shows up and asks you when you plan to pay, you know you've lost your standing. The code of conduct regarding money has to be pretty strict, for obvious reasons. We all stand on the edge of very slippery cliffs, where a man can start sliding and just disappear. Almost like drugs, things can get out of control very fast. People act like I'm a careless, whimsical man for playing: they think the same of all players. The truth is that we are very careful people, or we don't last long. Good fortune loves the bold and the careful. The more careful you are, the bolder you can be.

"So anyway, when I talk about gaming in this crazy town, I know what I'm talking about. You may laugh when I talk about the status of gaming, but have you ever looked around this whole city full of ugly architecture, where the 'Municipal Palace' looks like the 'Price Club' and the Cathedral itself looks like *indios* made it out of mud then left it under the rain? And have you ever noticed that there are only two beautiful old buildings in the whole town? And which ones? The Agua Caliente hippodrome and the jai alai *fronton*. Our landmarks. And did you ever think that both of them exist only for gambling in this fine city where gambling is supposed to be so illegal?

"Or look at the question this way, look at it. You see the government spending millions of dollars on tourism here in Baja California. Most of it goes into idiot projects that don't make money because they forgot to ask the gringos if they really wanted such a thing in the first place. And we end up with expensive, stupid monstrosities like 'Mexitlan' and wax museums. They spend a lot of money trying to prevent Mexicans from taking money out of the country into the United States. But do they ever think of making some legal gambling casinos here? Like Atlantic City, where it was illegal and evil until they made it legal and good to save their economy. Is that too simple to appeal to a politician? Can anyone really believe that gambling would be a hurtful influence on Tijuana? On *Tijuana*? This town was built on gambling and whoring. Now some Mercedes jockeys from the capital come here and want it all to be clean glass and sweet sunshine.

"What is wrong with gambling? That people spend too much money on it, like on liquor and women? So? We live with that, don't we? Many believe that gambling continues to be prohibited because of certain other powerful sectors with interest in gambling. Do I have to mention Jorge Hank Rhon, a very rich and powerful *chilango* whose uncle is the Secretary of Tourism? Should I point out that he owns both of those two nice buildings? In addition to all of these betting books all over Baja California? There is the thought that since he controls all legal gambling, and is powerful enough to influence the laws, that he must like things as they are. You talk to people who say, 'What is this rich young socialite doing living in an ugly pueblo like Tijuana, when he could be a big shot in a big town like Mexico?' Maybe because Baja and the border are the future and his family may be looking to take it over, make it richer than Mexico. And what is their main interest here? The only games in town. So, this talk is around. Not in newspapers of course—read any issue of *Zeta* and you might see why. So maybe you'd better think it over well before you say something like that. Journalists who badmouth Hank Rhon have been known to end up as cheap martyrs, you know.

First a man tells me he might bore me and then it turns out just talking to him is dangerous.

"Well, I was teasing you. Nobody really knows whether Hank Rhon has terminal relationships with writers, but every idiot thinks they know. Theories like that have a few faults if we look at them closely. For one thing, it could be of great advantage to Hank Rhon to have more gambling, which he could control if he wanted to. Would he rather see a million people from San Diego take their money to Las Vegas than lose a few local customers from his dog races? The races are not even making money. He would probably love to diversify. No, I don't think it's Rhon's fault, I don't think. Maybe it is. Who knows? What odds would you give?

"Then there are those who say that the government is afraid that gambling would bring in the Mafia. Does it really make sense that the PRI would be afraid of the Mafia? Is a lion afraid of a tiger? Our government shoots it out with the petroleum union, down in Playas you can't even park because the place is full of big cars that belong to drug traffickers, the country is full of DEA gringos trying to break our balls. . . and you think making millions of dollars is a problem because of the Mafia, you think? ¡*Ay, por favor*! The truth is, it would be hard for a lot of people to distinguish between the Mafia and the PRI. It would be interesting to see a war between those two, though. I guess I'd take the Mafia at eight to five. They'd probably run things smoother anyway. You want to see a clean, efficient, crime-free town, don't go to Mexico City, go to Las Vegas.

"You also hear that the government doesn't want games because they harm the people. Not from anybody with any intelligence, of course. That is not the way governments think or act. They say it's out of concern for the people, they don't want the people throwing their money away. Though they don't mind taxing us and throwing our money away without even giving anyone a hope or a thrill. It's ridiculous. You walk back into Mexico from San Ysidro and before you even get past the *taxistas* there's an open air Caliente betting book. Incredible, really. A shabby little taco stand with beat-up tables right in the filthy sidewalk full of poor people selling junk. . . and they have five televisions showing race odds and results. To attract foreign dollars? I don't really think so. What gringo is going to sit and bet on a sidewalk full of unwashed hustlers? You look who's betting—the people. Beggars are sitting there watching the Santa Anita results. Yet this is legal. Those people wouldn't be allowed into a casino even if they wanted to go. So much for the kindly government protecting the masses, eh? And take a look around and see how most people in Mexico hazard their money. The lottery. Millions and millions of pesos. Always several games at once, always new ones. And who runs these games? The government. The PRI has their hands on a million dollar monopoly and isn't thinking very much about letting anyone else put their spoon into it. That much is pretty obvious.

"It's the same game in California. They say gaming is illegal, but you can find places to play cards for money there, can't you find them? There's a place right on Broadway in Chula Vista. The Indians even have a real Casino out there at Viejas. Have the Mafia come in to take over, have they? And you will notice that the newspaper has all the data and statistics about the Superbowl, and one very prominent number is 'Caliente Line'. That's illegal, too, right? But they always mention it. They have Nick the Greek on the *tele* giving his unique athletic perspective on every big game, you notice. They've even got a 'money line' where you wager straight against the wager. Why have a money line if there's no money? Millions of dollars, not really legal, right? But evil casinos and open books would corrupt?

"To me personally it doesn't matter. The people lose, I win. If all the games were illegal, I'd make my money on illegal games. All I care about is luck. They talk about luck being a woman, a beautiful lady. Well, luck is a slut, really. As capricious as a she-goat. She leaves you when you most need her then roars up on you when you don't have enough money, or the other players don't have enough, to really take advantage. You read about these things in Las Vegas where some farmer wins a million dollars the first time he plays a slot machine. Thousands of people putting their whole life into faithfully supporting the temples of luck and she gives it up to some drooler who just walked in the door. And the guys in Las Vegas make sure you read about it. They want you to know what a drunken little whore luck is, because they are her pimps, that's what they are.

"But there's no mistaking luck—it's like carrying an electrical charge. Like having the power to command the world. It's a sexual feeling, a male feeling. Gambling is deep in the blood of Mexicans. Have you thought of the relationship between the jai alai *fronton* and the Aztec ball court? Now there's a little morsel of our national heritage; the original Mexican national sport. Every one of the big ruins—Chichen Itza, Bonampec, Palenque—they had a those big stone ball courts. The archeologists will tell you all about how the game was played. It's mysterious to me how they would know it all since there was no writing in those days but to hear them tell it they've got the rule book right in front of them and can tell you who drew a yellow card for being off-side and who quit during the season to go play for Argentina or Royal Madrid.

"But maybe they're right, maybe the whole idea was to hit the ball only with the buttocks and to hit it through that little stone donut up on the wall. Like butt basketball. So far the sages haven't published any box scores, but it must have been even lower-scoring than *futbol*. So maybe if anybody actually managed to score a ring, they got excited enough to stop the game while everybody in the numbered seats stripped down and gave all their clothes and jewelry to the player who scored. And the spectators were the royalty, the cabinet officials of the day; like a bunch of PRI *chilangos*, so they'd be covered with gold and all those women undressing would be the most beautiful women in the country. Not bad winnings at all. And not really all that different from today, come to think of it. Except now they have to score a lot of goals to get the clothes and jewels and the automobile. And they only get the naked beauties one or two at a time. And one other little difference. . . the losers died. Claim stakes, you might call it. It must have made it more interesting for everybody involved. And it shows the kind of patrimony we have, a people who these days are not allowed to play cards for money or bet on some stupid chickens.

"Since you're so curious and *simpática*, I'll tell you my dream. Over at the hippodrome they've got a "Six Pack" exacta, the old "Five Ten." You have to pick six winners, but the thing is that if nobody wins the prize, it's kept until the next week. So it keeps getting bigger. Understand? The normal betting is mutual. The everyone is wagering against each other. So if a thousand people each wager one hundred thousand pesos on a race, the winner would get a million pesos. Minus what the track takes. Probably about half. And what the taxes take, even worse.

"But if the prize is kept over another week, then you have two million pesos, and the next week you have three.

Three million more than the betting is sharing. So I could go to the book and buy up all the chances—a guaranteed win. Of course it would cost a lot. With ten dogs in each race, there would be one million possibilities. But you'd be 'winning' even more millions. This has happened before with these progressive purses. Ten years ago some guys from Texas walked into the jai alai *fronton* in Miami with around three and half million dollars in their briefcases and bought all the tickets to their exacta. The purse had reached almost seven million, so they made around four million dollars. Pretty good pay for a mornings work, in my unstudied opinion. Any time the prize exceeds the amount required to buy the tickets, there's a chance to do such a thing. There's a chance at Agua Caliente, but they won't admit it. Or are too arrogant to see it. That would be my life dream, to just buy up a winning like that. To run no risk at all, to cheat on luck the way that bitch cheats on us. But probably I'd see the opportunity and not be able to take advantage of it. That's the way life is. The way luck is. And I really can't complain. My luck has kept me alive so far.

"If you think my attitude is inconsistent, think about this: the reason people like gambling is because it is definite. In your normal life everything is uncertain, true? It all depends on somebody else, or you never get a final answer. You know what I'm saying: the election recount is being protested, the chance of rain is forty percent, your husband might just be tired instead of in love with somebody else, the judge suspends sentence but withholds bail pending an evaluation, analysts interpret the loss of oil revenues as an increase in the decrease of future prices which is such good news we shouldn't mind paying a little more. There is never any yes or no, never any right or wrong.

"It seems to be worse in the United States, maybe that's why they have more gambling and bigger lotteries. Over there everything has a warranty or insurance or some ridiculous lawsuit. Nobody knows how long a life sentence is or how many times you can marry somebody until death may part you. They can't even legally decide if someone is a man or a woman anymore. They freeze people so they aren't really dead yet. Look at Korea, Vietnam, the Gulf. . . they don't even know if they won their wars. So the people need something that is definite, that's either black or white. They talk about gaming 'addicts', but they're just people who can't accept it when they lose and don't believe it when they win. Believe me, you're going to see more play here in Mexico in the future because we're going that same way. Our whole lives are a big question and we probably never know if we did it right or not.

"But when you wager on games, you either win or lose. It's a goal or no goal, red or black, dead or alive. You can argue, but you can't change it. There's stress in playing, but for me there's also a sort of calm. Where else short of a coffin are things absolute? Not even in the Church. Maybe your wife can pray you out of purgatory, but let's see her pray you out of betting on the wrong dog. Sometimes I feel it very strongly that when I'm playing things are real; a simple, well-planned universe of good moves and bad moves. When I stop and go outside, the world out there is a cheap, stupid fake where nothing makes any sense and nobody agrees on the rules and nobody knows where they stand."

PRIDE GAMES

His eyes are old and still, his hair is dull gray. The way he sips a brandy that appeared without being ordered and stubs a Cuban cigar to punctuate his opinions reminds me of the coughing, chain-smoking old cynic on "*Que Nos Pasa*". But he's no cynic; he will weigh any proposition, perhaps defend it with a wager. He has money, and everyone knows his money came from winning wagers.

He is dressed like a businessman but with an elegance that isn't noticeable until his movements show the quality of his material. The tailoring is not the latest, the fabric is worn a little with an older man's gentle neglect, the gold Ronson lighter and Patek watch are worn, but everything is of top quality. He pretends to be of culture and education, but his speech is too much of the streets; he adds an "s" to his second person preterits, saying "*perdistes*" or "*supistes*" in a way that marks him as a border person lacking formal schooling. But he is also obviously a gentleman and a veteran.

Everyone in the Owner's Club at the hippodrome treats him with respect, the other players all go out of their way to greet him. Across the Boulevard at the Hot Tip restaurant, he takes a table that is obviously "his" and the waitresses calls him "Don Faustino". In his red leather booth under the round stained glass ceiling cupola, he is a personage who receives the attentions and admirations of other men who wager money. Nobody actually kisses his ring. But he has won for years, at all the games in town, so they probably would kiss his ring if he would let them. We can see that this is a man who could tell much about the arts of wager. But he doesn't want to.

"Not that it's any secret," he says. "The numbers, techniques, strategies; all of that is the easy part, advertised and published in books. That's for beginners. The real game is something from the heart. Well, not really from the heart. Nor from other organs you often hear mentioned. But from somewhere very close to the basic humanity. Risking everything important on something stupid just for the excitement, wanting something for nothing. . . what could be more human than that? It has nothing to do with money, it has nothing to do with luck. It's about a view of the world, about taking a conscious role in fortune and fate. About turning life from a struggle into a game".

Don Faustino is one gambler who does not believe that there exists such a thing as luck.

"Luck is a myth, really. It comes from drawing long-run conclusions from short-run observations. If you toss a coin forever, it will show the head fifty percent of the time. If the eagle comes up five straight times, you'd call it remarkable. If the eagle comes up when you've bet on the head, you'd call it bad luck. Professionals win money by superior knowledge of the games, that is all that happens. People who pick horses by their cute names don't understand that other people can evaluate them intelligently and have a better chance of knowing what they will do. That's all you need to win money; to have a better chance over a long time."

Neither does he believe that dog racing or jai alai are sports.

"Horse racing is a sport. And beautiful, an art really. Not that you can see much of it on television. But dogs? Who would go see these neurotic dogs run if there were no betting? The jai alai players are not sportsmen, they are like human greyhounds or roulette balls that merely produce results to wager on. Football is a sport. You see stadiums of half a million people yelling, killing each other for the love of their team, you see men giving their all for the love and glory of it. That's a sport. Even horses run for some noble reason. These dogs chasing a fake rabbit. . . doesn't it seem like a strange kind of race?"

I think that all racing is a little strange, really. All the effort, all the money. And what does it signify? Don Faustino shrugs, taps his cigar into an ashtray and says, "I'll tell you about some strange racing. Then you tell me what it signifies.

"I am originally from Tepic, Nayarit, and used to spend much of my time at the lake of Santa Maria del Oro. The lake fills a volcano crater and the water is very pure, almost sterile. It's a rather mystical place, really. That's where I spent my summers, and where I learned about magic and sex and luck. But it took me all my life to know what I'd learned.

"Strange, I don't know why I said that. My memories get more fanciful each time I remember them. By the time I die my whole history will be a fantasy. But you know, the lake was the place where we boys ran together and came of age, doing all the tribal things boys do. Every day was a race, a contest, a wide-open risk.

"One summer we discovered a great game: we would drop large round rocks off the end of a dock, then take as deep a breath as we could, jump in and grab a rock to hold us down while we ran across the sand bottom of the lake. For me, there was nothing ever like it, racing along down there, pushing hard to move through the water, everything distorted but with light breaking all around in waves. Everything was silent and slow motion, it wasn't a race of speed. The idea was, you'd run until you ran out of air. It was the best game I'd ever played at that time.

"It reminded me of a story about the Incas that I read as a boy, probably in some book from school. According to the story, the Incas had a special death to allow the most valiant and respected of their enemy captives to fly straight to the heart of the sun. They called them the Royal Condors. They would strip the man naked and stand him on a wide field facing into the sunset. A priest would step up behind him with an obsidian knife and suddenly slit the skin between his ribs, then reach in and pull out his lungs, which would stick out under his shoulders like wings. Then he would run to his death with honor. Run into the sun until he ran out of breath.

"It's the eternal classic race against death; the faster you run, the sooner you get there. Life against breath, running against your wind. It really laid its grips on my imagination, I'll tell you. But I'll have to be honest: if I'd been there I'd have been making some side bets. You know, to make it interesting.

"I used to picture those condors of the sun while I ran along under water, leaning over the rock and hugging it for the weight to push each step, feeling my lungs bursting for air.

I would try to run until I died or passed out, but I never could. Things would get very weird and wavy, but I always ended up dropping the rock and heading for the air as fast as I could. I told my friends about the condors, but they couldn't see it. All they knew was, it was fun to run on the lake bottom. To me, it was a game for sun kings.

"We found out that we could stay under water longer if we were almost asleep. I suppose the metabolism is slower when you first wake up. We would sleep on the dock at night and when we first woke in the morning we would just roll off into the water, just sink without moving, trying not to really wake up. I've stayed under almost three minutes like that, my personal record. Of course we would bet on who could stay under longer or run farther. A strange race; not how fast you could go but how far. Boys: we would bet on anything. I enjoyed it even then, but now it seems sad that only money could make the best things in youth exciting. I wonder if any Incas bet on those human condors. I'll bet they did.

"Thinking about the lake, about those times, I remember how it was in the early mornings when the sky was a little light but the sun hadn't come over the edge of the crater. Very eerie light through the steam off the water. And even stranger underwater because the light was so diffused. It didn't form ripples on the bottom like normal sunlight—it seemed to come from everywhere at once. I would float up from an underwater sunrise into a misty white world. I'd swim out until I couldn't see the dock and it was like not even being born. I'd float there, naked, in a world like a white egg half full of water, half full of smoky light. As soon as the dock disappeared, my vision would start to play tricks. I'd start hallucinating things until the sun burned through the mist. Not like dreaming, more like colors and visions. Very sexual, as you can imagine. I was a teenager.

"Once one of our friends brought a big metal sign out onto the dock. It was a steel disk almost two meters across, painted like a big cap from a bottle of Pacifico beer. We wanted to take it home, have the biggest beer bottle top in town, but it was too big for the car and anyway it was rusty and had some bullet holes in it. Finally we threw it in the lake, hoping it would skip like a stone, but it was too heavy. But it skimmed out several meters before it started to sink. It was just a few millimeters under the surface, moving slow as a big turtle under the water, moving away from us, sinking so slow we could barely see any movement. It curved away from us and finally we couldn't see it anymore. We talked about it awhile, wondering if we could have ridden it like a magic carpet in the water, how we could have gotten on without upsetting it. Then we lost interest and started fishing. Later, maybe fifteen or thirty minutes, one of my friends jumped up and said, 'Look! Look! It's coming back!' True; the big bottle cap was coming right toward us, still barely moving, now half a meter deep. It went by like a manta ray and we could even read it, '*Tome Pacífico, Nada Más.*' There was something very wonderful about it, that big sign sliding along under us like it had its own mind and plans. I tried to bet that it would come back by, but nobody would take it. I finally got a bet that it would be close enough to read at least twice more. And it was. It passed by five more times, always the same speed, always deeper, always just a little farther out in the lake. When my friends went in to cook the fish, I stayed and watched for the sign. I kept thinking I saw it hovering along down there, but I couldn't be sure. How many times did it come around again? I'll never know for sure. And you don't know why I'm wasting your time with these crazy stories."

It's a beautiful story, *señor*, the images are magical. "But nothing to do with your reporting, true?"

At this point, I wouldn't want to bet with you on that. "Very astute. Because. . . well, because, it's a sort of parable, you know. I have thought of it many times. The first time the sign passed by us it seemed like a miracle—round and gold as the moon, sliding under the water like a fish seeking flies. Could such a thing happen twice? Should you hazard money on a miracle? But after the second pass, none of us would have bet on the proposition; we knew the mechanism now, the cycle behind that event. But what if someone else had come by and seen it passing silently beneath the pier? How much would they hazard that such a thing could never happen twice? I can see that you hear what I am saying. You might wager about eclipses with a savage Indian, but not with an astronomer, true? Thus it is. There are games of chance like throwing dice, and there are games of knowledge in which those who know the rhythms and cycles play on those who don't. Ninety-five people bring all the money to the racetrack, five people take most of it away. And the one who makes the most is the owner of the racetrack.

"It's not so different with dice or cards, either. The ones who know the mathematics and the large cycles win money from those who are concentrated only on the drama and trauma of the moment. They say, 'Ay, the double zero! When will that happen again?' And a man they don't even notice says, 'Once every thirty four times.' That man is the student, the scientist of life. He's taken fate into his hands and examined it. The others, who are just living their life? They aren't really living at all.

"Ah, what am I talking about here, chirping like an old cricket? About putting money on the most marvelous things of my life, making them mean as little as money. Now I can see what that did to me. Nothing was wonderful enough without some money or pride being wagered. Is that crazy? Of course we bet on sex as soon as it was practical. The first girl I ever had, I had bet my friends I could get her in less than a month. I don't know which excited me more, my first taste of woman or winning the bet. Very similar feelings, power and gladness. You want to thank someone or something, you want everybody to see you and know what you have won, what you are feeling. Powerful. That's how sex makes me feel and that's how winning makes me feel. Losing used to make me feel impotent and cheated, desperate to place another bet to change my luck and feel like a winner. Two out of three, four out of seven, two thousand out of four thousand and one. Double or nothing. Never settle for losing. Until you've lost everything and have to go home.

'Winning is the greatest feeling in the world, maybe better than sex. But the more powerful motive is not wanting to lose. It's like... Well, winning a woman is exciting, but losing your woman is absolute hell. There's no comparing the impact on your heart and your life. So every race, every cut of the cards, every toss of the coin reveals either orgasm or death. It's like movies or *telenovelas*, really. Life condensed to essentials, with all the water and fat boiled away. Life may be short, it seems like a lot of time to kill when you're bored. There's the secret of gaming for you right there... you might be winning or you might be losing, but you aren't bored."

But you're at the hippodrome watching dogs run without making bets, you've mastered all the games in your life, mastered money. Aren't you bored? "Fortunately, I've found a new game. One I haven't yet mastered. It's keeping me young, and interested. It makes about five years now I've been playing poker. Mostly in Las Vegas. It's been frustrating and a little humiliating, which is a sure sign that a man is growing and learning, not being bored to death. I'm used to thinking of myself as the guy who knows, the *chingón*. But up there, with those guys, I'm like a little baby. It took me awhile to find that out—they don't let you know it right away. Especially because you don't want to know it. But it's the case. The first time a couple of guys in a suite in the Tropicana took about nine hours to pluck me of a month's worth of Caliente winnings I was ready to kill somebody. Principally myself. I just couldn't believe that a bunch of asinine gringos in silly clothes could take down a sharp fellow like me. But I had to face up to the humiliation. And go back for more.

149

"I'm usually very practical about losses. You have to be when it's your business. I think the reason I lost my head was the same reason I want to be a poker winner. It's a man's game. Not just mathematics and espionage, like selling insurance or something. It's a game you play with your manhood. The only man's game, really.

"I've been studying the probabilities on filling hands and all of that. In blackjack that's all you need to know. (Along with luck, if we're granting there is such a thing.) But in a poker game you're playing with your face, your posture, your attitude, your *cojones*, that's all. Your playing with your life, who you are.

"The bluff. That single aspect is the genius of poker. It's really what's behind the whole macho element of the game. In what other game can you hold the high hand and yet lose because you are stupid or frightened or practical? Or have nothing and win anyway. . . with only you knowing what you have done?

"The more I learn about poker the more I learn about being a man. If winning a hand was just a matter of having the most points. . . Let me compare it to physical machismo, being a tough guy. If it was just a matter of fighting skills and muscles, there would be no need to fight, there'd be tournaments like judo and boxing, everybody would have a ranking and that would be that. But no, the tough guy in the *cantina*, the *matón*, is not so much an expert in fighting as in bluffing. He walks in and stares everyone down. That's not to say he's not dangerous. You want to find out, just call his bluff.

"It's the same way with sexual machismo, true? Women don't know what you've got. And it doesn't matter, because it's not what you've got but what they think about it. Otherwise they'd just measure everyone and pass out women in order of size. So a man is signaling to women, letting them know he is a straight flush to the ace—full house, king over queen. There are no results posted, you bluff and they either lay down or fold. Bluffing is what a man does. And women? I wouldn't know. I think it's different with women. What you see is what there is—beauty, childbearing, sex. Women really don't have to do anything to be somebody, it seems. But I wouldn't really know.

"There's more elegance in poker. Where are the *cojones* in betting something like roulette? You pile up money and make a guess. You drop big stacks of chips, you take your losses like a man and people will be impressed. But impressed at what? If you're rich you can just keep betting until you win. There's no pride, no shame, no guts, no soul. Maybe you are betting all you have. *¡Ay, chingada!* But so what? How much do you have to wager on a coin toss to make it interesting, to bring your character into the question? You could play roulette by flipping coins. You can program a computer to play blackjack. To win, even, if the house is playing fair. But a computer can't play winning poker. There has to be a person there, there has to be a man to make decisions, to read the faces, to advertise confidence, to risk something of himself. So when I win, I know I'm the winner and when I lose I have nobody to blame but myself. When it comes to real games, luck is an illusion and has nothing to do with anything. Except I guess I should admit I'm lucky to be alive."

LOVE GAMES

Yes, you would say that the way he walks is very sexual and feline; more so than even athletes or dancers. Even though he supports himself with a cane. I wonder about these professional gaits; the characteristic baseball strut, the boxer's glide, the stooped shuffle of basketball. Is it muscles trained by certain movements, or graces learned by feeling the eyes of crowds? This man's movements, which seem designed to be devastating to women, come from a long career of dancing with bulls and flirting with that instant when the satin swirl of the dance collapses into the brute animal of death.

I am restrained from giving his name, although it is well-known. I met him at a *pista* party at the house of my friend, a woman who has known him for years. Lacking the permissions of a formal interview, I should only report his remarks as from an anonymous acquaintance. Like the other men in this story, though the others are anonymous in the actual life. I think it's better this way, because what interests us here has nothing to do with his fame, nor even his skills. We all face our vital risks, our blessed victories and our ultimate defeats: we might not experience them in pavilions of favor, but in those common interior places where we are all heroes, all anonymous, all immortal.

He walks with a cane because a month earlier he couldn't walk at all. Because a month before that he had what he calls a "perchance" in the Tijuana *Toreo*; a bull perchanced to catch him on its horns, cutting deep into his thigh muscles and thorax, then shaking and trampling him, breaking skin, flesh, ribs and knees. Now he is healing, trying to get command of his body so he can fight again. He is forty-five years old, and most of his colleagues say he would be crazy to return to fight. I'm afraid I feel the same way.

"I suppose I'm in no position to argue with that," he says, "taking into account what has happened. I feel like I can still fight. But I felt that way in the arena until suddenly my leg didn't move fast enough and I was on the bull's face. Then it was too late; the pain of the first puncture hurt me so bad and what I felt in my stomach and chest had me frightened. . . then he got me again. I had never imagined being gored. Never. Certainly nothing like this one, tearing me up like this. I'll tell you how I felt; I felt very badly hurt. A few seconds shaking around on the face of a furious bull is a long enough time; then I had to spend forever in the clinic, hurting. Those animals have no respect for a man's years and that's the sad truth."

The list of injuries is a long one, from knees to the top of the head. His body is a map of scars. He says that the scars could be studied to determine the size of the bull and how it behaves at the time of killing. I thought briefly of Kafka's "Penal Colony", where the condemned man deciphers his wounds to learn the nature of his crime. But he rejects retirement, rejects easier paths such as caping calves. He is already planning a return to the arena on a full matador card, even after these accidents have left him scarred, broken, and aware of the full extent of fear. This might be from heroism or egomania in a man, or from the fear of admitting fear. In this case the reason is simpler.

"I'm poor. I have not done very well with my money, and have had problems with managers, impresarios, and bull-breeders. It's useless to complain about that; I'm a grown man. But I have a family that I love and no money to support them, no patrimony to leave my children. I'm no daredevil, but under these circumstances, a man has to be a bit of an adventurer." So he speaks of returning to wager his health—even his life—against money.

"You could call it, that I suppose. I don't see it as a wager, just doing my art, my career. How can I compute my chances? It's too simple to say that I'm risking my life. I'm a *matador*, I expect to die on my wheels, not watching television. So are there odds that I will die? What are the odds that you will die? I compute them at one hundred percent for both of us. But hopefully I will not die in pain with my tripes in the dirt."

What if he should return to the arena and be opened up again by the bull?

"If I can't do this job, obviously I would have to quit, find some job to do with my wife to make money for my children. But since I think I can continue, there is only one way to find out. I am surprised by people who say I should walk away from bulls because they might kill me. What else is bullfighting, anyway?

153

"Without somebody going onto the horns now and then, where would the mystique come from? It's the mystical part of the entire pageant, what men burn candles and tell rosaries and guard superstitions over. They are not praying not to be gored: I think that the young, especially, actually anticipate that experience. Like a virgin anticipating her deflowering. They are praying that if they are gored they won't die, or won't die in some ugly way. In fact, I have begun to think that I might be praying for that myself. Not to die in a manner too stupid or ugly or ungracious. Like the bull does.

"At the ultimate level of this diversion, that is the real balance. The bull can only die like a beast, never with the grace and beauty of a man, with paintings done and women mourning. He is just meat. On the other hand, what has he got to lose compared to me? He has always been meat, but I have a soul in the bargain. That's what nobody but a *torero* can ever really understand. The moment of truth doesn't come at the tip of a sword, it comes at the tip of a horn.

"Fighting the bull is only a question of skill, of the mind and spirit controlling mere animal flesh. Technique. In time it requires fine bulls to keep it challenging. But when you have made a mistake, when the bull takes control. . . when the horns enter your body it is all so very suddenly a question of luck, or fate or whatever you want to call it. The place we keep our prayers and lucky pendants and good deeds against. In just seconds big, rough events occur in places where only millimeters separate life and death. You want to talk about truth, I give you the moment when the hard, sharp world comes inside of you and with no respect for your belief or your person. It's also the moment all the people wait for.

"You know that. You know it's not the bull's blood that excites them, that makes it so macho and sexually exciting for the fine ladies. It's my blood that does that. Otherwise, I'd be just an athlete, just a cowboy. I carry the real import of this sport right here in my veins and there is nobody to help me keep it there. If I don't, the seats will get more than their money's worth, right? They'll get something special they'll never forget, like catching a home run ball. It'll be their lucky day."

VII. FAITH, APHRODISIACS, AND FREEZE-DRIED BLOOD

Just as the purest form of the Mexican diet is very often found in the rude conditions of the streets, some of the humblest and most exotic products sold in Tijuana are the herbal, folk, and "grandmother" cures sold by migrant sidewalk vendors. At times of fairs and religious festivals they can be found lining the streets along with the other entrepreneurs who spring up with stands full of plastic hardware and Chinese-made tools.

Maybe a miniature Indian woman so old she barely speaks Spanish will sit on a worn blanket covered with dishes of shredded bark and leaves she has gathered in the southern rain forests. Or there might be a timid young mother nursing a new child and offering small paper sacks scrawled with spells, pictures of the organs they promise to relieve, or emblems of saints. A certain weathered *ranchero* is almost always seen with fresh-cut desert herbs and skinned, headless rattlesnakes dried into stiff loops.

The herbs usually have native names that are outlandish even to Mexicans and can be counted on for relief of vague symptoms that might include "female complaints", loss of love, and tumors. Endorsements include personal testimony, generations of folk wisdom, and much pointing to

157

saintly names written on the sacks while making signs of the holy cross or the evil eye. Of course, opportunities to experience these "divine gifts of purest nature" are too unpredictable for those who don't wish to wait until the next Festival of Guadalupe to purchase an ounce of *tlanchichinole* or dried viper. But fortunately for those who haven't properly planned their infirmities and thus have to content themselves with purchasing their cures over the counters of more conventional establishments, Tijuana has a wide range of such shops, each specialized in certain types of tastes and organismic shortcomings. Places with names like *Centrál Botánica, Farmácia Homeopática* or *Centro Naturalista* sell herbs, health food, "grandmother cures", and sexual enhancements. But they play a much more important role in the national metabolism than food, medicine, or even sexuality—they sell magic. Or what might be called applied faith.

Some of these botanic stores resemble San Diego "health food" stores and sell foods like wheat germ and whole grain bread (*pan integral* as it's called here). Others stack herbal remedies beside the type of products sold in conventional pharmacies. In Tijuana these are often selected towards such medicines as strong sedatives, rejuvenation formulae and cures for cancer or sterility that are not available in the United States, where the line between the medical canon and unorthodox cures is more sharply drawn than here.

The entire idea of "alternative medicine" is much less clear in Mexico than in the United States, which is why people cross the border for drugs and treatments that are illegal on the other side. There are two perspectives on that matter: some denounce exploitation and fakery while others reclaim against narrow-mindedness and suppression of health by powerful interests. To me it seems that in the United States science is like a powerful floodlight, like those observed lighting the border. There is light and there is darkness: the shadows have sharp edges. In Mexico, the official sanction is more like a bonfire whose light shades off gradually into darkness and casts softer shadows that flicker and dance.

Some shops, like the *Centrál Botánica de California*, sell very little except herbs, but every herb you could think of. It is like a clean white warehouse full of herbs and dried plants. In fact, it looks something like a clinic, and I find it amusing and a little frustrating that all those aromatic herbs are sealed tightly in glass jars and stacked in alphabetical order: their cures are all genuinely organic and botanic, but there should be so much more to smell!

On the other hand, as part of a large network of herbal growers, gatherers, and vendors, they are very serious and knowledgeable about herbs and provide literature and advice on their uses. Which is fortunate because it could take years to sort out the variety of folk cures available. It is very helpful to approach these tall walls of odd-looking dried plants knowing that *cuachalate* is good for ulcers, *azocopaque* for rheumatism and gout, *sihupatle* for painful menstruation, *tlanchalahua* for burning fat while dieting, and *pimpinela* for combating dandruff, hair loss and follicle damage. But in what doses, and by what preparation? And what if they are taken together? It's like walking into a drug warehouse wondering which color pill might do some good.

Centrál Botánica de California emphasizes their selection of plants from all over Mexico and even the world, but some of the herbs are from local sources. Eucalyptus leaves, for instance, which can be picked for free in much of San Diego, become exotic imports when sent to other Mexican cities. *Guata*, a kidney remedy, and *alcachofa* for cirrhosis and other liver diseases, are regional desert plants that *Centrál Botánica* gathers not only for their local store, but to ship throughout the Republic. Even humbler is the powerful diuretic weed *la gobernadora*, which grows alongside highways throughout the northern part of the state. Local people harvest it during its flowering season and it, too, becomes a state export. *Damiana* is the most famous Baja California herb, not so much for its curative properties or the liquor made from its leaves, but because of its reputation as an aphrodisiac.

Which approaches another important sideline of the herbal shops. Man, after all, does not live solely by bread; not even integral bread. When the flesh starts to fail the spirit—or vice versa—semi-medicinal avenues can be attractive and most of the *botánicas* stock as many sexual tonics and invigorants as can be found. There are entire walls covered with various formulations of Ginseng. Preparations of exotic Asiatic herbs like *ma huang* and *gotu kola* promise virility if not actual passion. Almost all such stores and all drug stores carry patent potency potions like Zumba. Such preparations are almost exclusively in support of male vigor. Willing women are considered a bit too sexy as it is and any lack of response they might experience would best be cured by more vigorous male attention. Naturally a cure for female unwillingness would be a best-seller, but so far little has been reliably established on that frontier.

Though there are impressive claims. A male friend once pointed out to me a product called Gerovital, another popular Tijuana drugstore item since it is illegal in the United States. He told me he and his wife, both of them in their middle fifties, had bought some and tried it out right there at the store. By the time they got home they were both frantic. They left a trail of clothes into the bedroom and fell upon each other like what he called, "adolescent animals in heat".

That demonstration, as you might imagine, convinced them to buy more Gerovital, even at a price of over twelve dollars per dose. But it never again worked the same magic as the first application and they quit buying it. He thinks the initial effects were due to anticipation, or to belief conditioned by the decision to spend the money. He mentioned something called "the placebo effect". What that means is: if a person truly believes that a medicine will help him, it will. Having been given this respectable name, the principle becomes very scientific. Perhaps it's just my ignorance of both medicine and mysticism that makes me unable to differentiate "placebo effect" from superstition. Or from a healing through true faith.

This "placebo" idea seems to describe a space between the medical and the mystical that refuses to be clearly defined; a space in which the great majority of the naturalistic boutiques do most of their business. And in that space, in the collection of *"productos místicos"*, there can be seen a spiritual portrait of the local people.

A favorite product is *"Legítima Agua Espiritual"*; plastic bottles of water to be used in blessing, cleansing, or attracting fortune. *Sanctísima Muerte* water, which seems to be a big seller, offers success, strength, and fortune, especially if conscientiously applied in a nine-day program. Obviously the appeal of this product among Catholic people is drawn from the insinuations of the *Novena* and the charged words "Holiest Death", just as the acceptance of the powers in water is conditioned by the use of Holy Water in the Church. Many of the waters also use the names of Saints, especially such as St. Antonio Martyr, Santa Marta and St. Cipriano, who bring fortune or protect from witchcraft. Other waters invoke "Macho Garlic", "Adam and Eve", "The Buddha Divine Grace", "Against Witches", "Just Judge", "Double Good Luck Thirteen", "Peace in the Home", and "Come To Me".

Another form of magical application is the "Legitimate Powerful Powder"; an envelope of dust which can be sprinkled on the wet hands, the body, perhaps even the bed and clothes of the intended enchanted. The powders are simple and easy to use, so there are many of them. "The Black Hen" protects against curses and the evil eye. "Hunting Dog" will get rid of bad neighbors—unless, perhaps, they are "Black Hen" customers? More practical are "San Martin Caballero", which aids in business and financial success, and "Student Powder", which promises "ready brains and a clear mind". An envelope of

"Frog" allows a lover to "dominate the thoughts of the beloved and always have him captive"; "Kneel at my Feet", with its picture of a man kneeling in front of a temptress, indicates a form of love perhaps somewhat less pure.

The most bizarre of the powders, sold in "*La Guadalupana*", only blocks from the *Cuahuila* redlight district, features a silhouette of a prostitute leaning on a lamp post and the name "Woman X". On the back of the envelope, instead of more usual instruction, are several inscriptions. First a famous quote from the famous nun poetess Sor. Juana Inez: "Who is more guilty, she who sins for pay or he who pays for sin?"

Next a quote from Jesus Christ, "Let he who is without sin throw the first stone." Furthermore, the package notes, the Holy Church itself has said that, "Sin is Original".

"So firm your resolve, go ahead," the little packet concludes. "But put on this powder before you go to work." It would not require subtle psychology to assume that just reading the packet would provide a woman sinning for pay as much relief as whatever benefits the powder itself might provide. Certainly a bargain at only two thousand pesos each packet.

Many of the "Name" brands of waters and powders also appear as colored candles and incense—more examples of copying proven Catholic imagery—as well as soaps, and shampoos. The apparent idea is that if a name works it can be successfully franchised to other products; thus concept-marketing love, grace and fortune in the same manner as Oscar De La Renta or Ralph Lauren. There are even matches to strike for luck or protection and, certainly the latest technology in the ancient field of commerce, aerosol sprays. Just a touch of the button can soak a room, boudoir or automobile in the essential vibrations of St. Marta, St. Jude, or Holiest Death.

This combination of primitive magic and modern pressure technology is a good analogy to the ways in which faith seeps around and thorugh the boundaries of the world. I'm

162

sure many developed and enlightened Americans see the use of luck matches and saintly aerosols—apart from being damaging to the ozone—as childish and primitive, a little too charming to be absolutely laughable. But what's really on sale is faith, in a variety of strength and flavors. Many of those who mock superstition are only incapable of having or imagining faith. Which is also a lack of hope. And, for that matter, charity.

Magical thinking, especially about luck (a kind of magical concept in itself when you think of it: a name for a force beyond randomness) and romance (the most magical thinking of all) is still very prevalent at all levels of Mexican culture. When I was at the University I worked in a florist shop. Women customers would ask if I had a boyfriend and pass on little recipes to getting one through *magia blanca* with flowers. I sold a lot of white and red carnations that were used to make petal baths for bringing luck in love. And I got a lot of advice on using the petal water on a lucky day like Friday, thinking positive thoughts while soaking the petals, and consulting the phases of the moon.

Even more common are traditions of plants that bring luck. I remember when almost any business you visited would have a potted *albahaca,* given for luck by friends. Better yet, a *millonaria* with a coin (preferably gold) buried in the soil to bring wealth. In the older days, a garden with *albahaca, romero, ruda* and medicinal *salvia* would bring a wholesome spirit to the entire household.

The best-selling *Beauty Advice from Head to Toe* by Arturo Palacios, famous hairdresser to movie and music stars, has a great deal of advice that would be considered as much magical as herbal. For instance, he recommends cutting the hair at the full of the moon then planting the clippings under a plant that flowers or flows in the desired way so the hair will grow as the plant grows. It is amazing how many vain idiots blindly follow Palacios' advice, even though I can testify from personal experience that it doesn't work.

At another level, I could use the example of my own mother. She gave my older sisters nice flower names like Gladiola and Jacaranda. Then, after four girls with no boys, and two miscarriages, she started calling us after saints. And after only two of us, Ana and Monica, with saintly names she had Juan Jose. And after Marta, Tomás, Tonio, and Clara. What would you call such behavior? Superstition? Faith? Responsible Catholicism? Sympathetic magic? Call it what you will, a notable thing is that it worked. What would you call such results? I myself consider the path from the Holy Names to my mother's womb a little too complex to allow the drawing of facile conclusions.

Maybe this is the famous Latin tendency towards "magical realism". Having the disadvantage of being an actual *Latina*, rather than a New York literary critic, I'm not really sure what "magical realism" actually is. It seems to be a sort of infection which causes otherwise normal books suddenly to develop characters who are surrounded by butterflies. But the point of all these potions and lucky charms is the engineering of belief. Since belief is the strongest power in the world, the technology is potent, if shadowy and poorly-understood. What is important to the normal believer is to believe in something that works.

Which explains the confusion of images one finds in many of the *botánicas*, where you can see pyramids next to Buddhas next to crosses and ankhs. One dark store with a gypsy atmosphere of incense smoke has a meter-high statue of a bald Chinese Confucius or Lao Tse cast in solid red transparent plastic. It's quite grotesque, of course, but I could visualize it with a bulb inside it, making a warm red night light. That particular shop sells the ultimate in products for clients who want to spread their bets; little icons covered with pictures and statuettes of everything from the Virgin of Guadalupe to the third eye, from Saints to the Buddha, from horse shoes to Indian idols to lottery symbols to national flags. The shrines are covered with heat-shrunk plastic wrap to shield the fetishes inside from dust and other physical harm, perhaps so they can concentrate their powers on more important protections.

Obviously this is ignorant superstition at its most chaotic. But those little shrines are also a form of folk art, cultural realities that indicate that the Catholicism of Mexico is not as solid as many people believe it to be. In many ways we are as primitive as Africans and for a large percentage of Mexicans, Catholicism serves less as an absolute than as a central institution to organize whatever mob of credibility can be hung upon it. I'm not sure that the Mexican ability to believe in everything at once is inferior to a country like the United States in which most people appear to believe in nothing at all.

Apart from that, even the most objectionable and sacrilegious of this mixing of Catholic, native, and lost-and-found images is typical of the religion of the world, which is also not as solid as people think; less like banks or governments than like blurring urban languages and mutating fashions. The hybridization and cross-pollination of belief systems has been going on everywhere, forever. And the use of Catholicism as a host to sustain more primitive beliefs is nothing new at all. The most famous Catholic parasite is Voodoo. It is not widely known, but Voodoo practitioners must be Catholic communicants—even Papa Doc Duvalier, head of the only state in the world with Voodoo as the official religion, couldn't practice his own religion after he was excommunicated from the Catholic church.

A Latin American version of witchcraft and paganism hidden in Catholicism is *Santeria*, "saintcraft" very similar to Voodoo. *Santeria* is also a religion of possession—perhaps not al that different from the recent phenomenon of "channeling"—and it is also a parasite on Catholicism, like a tapeworm or the eggs of the cuckoo.

To a *santero,* the saints are just masquerades, faces the old African gods wear in the West, just as Negro people needed

165

to put on different faces and names in the new world. On a *santero* altar, a candle of Santa Barbara really represents Shango. Saint Lazarus and Saint Peter hide within them Yamaya, and Oggun. Matters of exact identity are of little import to gods who come down to earth and take over human bodies; speak with their mouths, rampage with their genitals, kill with their hands. A prayer book for the Seven Powers contacts the Gods. A call to Great Saint Peter is redirected to Ocha, orations to Our Lady of the Waters are heard by savage ears. The candles, the herbs, the blessed water, even the authentic holy prayers—all serve different masters in a religion that treats of blood, sensualism and power. To a Catholic, *santeria* is a blasphemous parasite that invades the bosom of the True Church. But to a *santero* the Church is merely a flavorless shell that protects and nurtures the spark of true faith within it, just as Zen Monks and Sufis see Buddhism and Islam as mere vehicles.

This is not to say that *Santeria* is common in Tijuana, although it does exist here and its adherents buy products from the *botánicas* I have mentioned. Even the white, sterile *Centrál Botánica* sells freeze-dried deer blood which can be used both as a cure for stomach pains and for occult purposes. They promise that it is as medicinally dynamic as fresh blood, but would it serve as well for occult purposes? I couldn't find any witches or vampires to testify, though one woman did whisper to me that the blood was not really from deer, but cattle. I certainly wouldn't have known the difference by examining the little brown nuggets, but I did find that they reconstituted very easily in hot water. Instant blood. I imagine that vampires would find it similar to instant coffee, the sacrifice in quality compensated by the convenience.

Similarly, they sell rattlesnake in gelatin capsules. Claimed to be just as good as the crude cadaver for purifying the blood, reducing tumors and ridding of acne. . . but do these capsules have any of the sexual potency so instinctively present in the stiff, taut-ribbed snakes? Who would you rather believe, the educated words of a white-suited expert or the naked, blatant sight of the flesh of a serpent in the hands of a weathered, ancient cowboy?

Because faith exists in many gray zones and shades: even Voodoo and *Santeria* are formalized religions with many followers who share the same beliefs and symbols, but there are thousands of similar blendings and heresies and minor "sects" with no name. A local *curandero* might do a cure through herbs or sacrificial magic, yet attribute the cure to Jesus or the Virgin. A devout woman might go to mass, buy small metal *milagros* in front of the cathedral to influence holy grace, stop by for some mystic powders to rearrange her health or love life, drink some Buddha Dream Tea before going to bed with a book on Zodiac Karma. The little shrink-wrapped shrines are sacred to some nameless impulse. This has also been the case around the world throughout time. When Christianity was introduced into India, the missionaries were pleased with how fast it was accepted, then horrified to realize that Hinduism, a huge, amorphous amoeba of a religion, was capable of swallowing up their teachings and converting Christ into the latest manifestation of Krishna.

And here in Mexico, where Octavo Paz once said that Mexicans believe in nothing except the lottery and the Virgin of Guadalupe, there are heretical evidences of cultural blending and appropriation in the *Guadalupana* cult. These are things a devout Mexican scarcely dares to think about—but there they are. One attack on the legitimacy of the virgin of Guadalupe has been widely read because it was authored by the Rius, Mexico's favorite cartoonist, satirist and polemicist. In comic book form, Rius sets out to show that the Guadalupe "myth" was actually a Catholic plot to convert the Aztecs and enslave the Mexican working classes with the opiate of religion. Rius, for all his other talents, is an atheist, Communist, vegetarian, feminist, and author of a self-teaching suicide manual. Aside from attacks on the Church itself, Rius relates interesting ideas about the succession of Gods in Mexico. The spot on Tepayac hill where the Virgin wanted her temple built was the site of an Aztec temple to Tonantzin, mother of Huitzipochitl, a Christ-figure in the Aztec religion. The Virgin took on various aspects of the Aztec goddess, including the date of her solstice celebration.

This is a fascinating area of scholarship, but Rius devotes most of his work not to exploring the similarities of Aztec and Christian concepts, such as the missionaries comparing the rain god Tlaloc to John the Baptist, but to collecting proofs that challenge the entire story of the Virgin appearing to a humble Indian and painting her image on his cloak to prove to Bishop Zumurraga that he should build a church on Tepeyac. He identifies—but how reliably?—the man who painted the cloak. He makes much of the switching of Church calendar dates to approximate pagan festivals, but we see the same thing with St. Valentine's day, and even Christmas— much less Easter, Lent, and Carnival, which are derived from the Equinox. He shows, with proofs virtually impossible to deny, that Bishop Zumurraga never mentioned the incident in his writing and was actually absent from Mexico when the vision took place.

So. Should I accept these proofs because they are documented? Renounce them because they are heretical? Or just continue believing or disbelieving that God's grace could rise out of Man's fakery, that the Christ could rise out of a manger, that health can rise out of a weed, that luck and romance can rise out of concentration on trivialities? In a world in which scientists, doctors, and governments disagree on the values and dangers of the food and medicines we consume things like faith, magic and love remain difficult to prove, but impossible to disprove completely.

And so we come again to the important and tiresome matter of proofs and facts, supposedly the very things that differentiate the sheep from the goats, the light from the darkness. Everybody wants faith in things unseen, but also everybody wants to see for themselves. How wide is the circle of light, how broad the umbrella of faith? Who among us understands even the simplest miracle?

As a Catholic, I believe that if a certain man says certain words he can convert ordinary wine and bread into the actual, literal blood and flesh of a man who died twenty centuries ago but it's certainly nothing I would try to prove to anyone. It is one of the oldest and most widely held beliefs in the world: scientifically ridiculous. So should I laugh at the superstitions of the ignorant? Or condemn them as inferior competitors of the true faith? Or sympathize with the odd perversions and contaminations we render to the spirit when we try to apply it to the weakness of the flesh?

Life, health and sanity are all circles of light surrounded by endless darkness. Perhaps it is in the twilight between the two that the nature of both become more clear to us. If we're going to have faith, we might as well have blind faith: if we're going to be realists, we might as well be a magical realists.

VIII. CRADLE OF WOLVES

My first thought was that I was mistaken: a woman like that does not find herself shopping in a supermarket in Tijuana. I don't know where she would live: Mexico City certainly, or Cancun or Acapulco. Somewhere glamorous, probably being waited on by muscular, oiled, naked slaves. But no, everybody in Mexico knows what Olga Breeskir looks like. In fairly intimate detail. She is a household word, a synonym for corporeal beauty and sexual desirability. And there she was, strolling through Comerciál Mexicana with cereal and vegetables and *leche nido* in her shopping cart. An even, *Dios mío*, some clothes! This is where famous sex symbols buy their clothing? Well, not that she's known for having clothes on. But what she does wear I would have thought were made from silk and metal thread by oversexed minimalist spiders from another planet.

My second thought was a deep flash of sheer, bright green envy. She is older than I am, has to be sixty. Why should I look like a grandmother when she looks like a teenaged gymnast? No matter why: *how*? Beyond that, isn't it a rebuke to justice that I should be chubby after a life of piety and hardship, while she walks through a forest of turned and admiring heads after a life of shamelessly displaying herself to the lusting eyes of men? But that starts to approach the justice of God hav-

171

ing made us the way we are, so I contain my envy, which eventually tames itself into admiration of just how beautiful and perfectly formed she is. And recently very dedicated to the Church and God, they say. I suppose I can only appreciate that life is nothing if not variety.

I chose that word slyly—in Mexico *variedad* means night club shows. If the word is not displayed outside of those *centros nocturnos* into which men disappear, it will be murmured or shouted by those empty-faced, oddly sexless men who guard the doors. It means, "women dancing on the stage" and hints at revelations and sin. The reality, it turns out after rigorous and courageous investigation, is both more and less than the flash of flesh.

I often get the impression that Americans think that Mexico is somehow wickeder than they are. That in Mexico, dark alleys conceal awful degradations involving the devaluated cheapness of life: dark, shameful things that would never occur in your more civilized country. Which is exactly the impression most Mexicans have of the United States.

To stay with the theme of *variedad*, of "girlie shows", of nakedness before the eyes of men, I have found that our *cantinas*—which I myself grew up seeing as dark, mysterious places steeped in iniquity and evil—are not even in the league with the American equivalent. This might have something to do with Catholicism, perhaps it is involved with women's liberation, perhaps it has to do with purely economic factors. Gringos always have bigger, better, shinier, more expensive things to entertain them.

But for whatever reasons, if I was a man I would go to the "titty bars" or "naked dance clubs" in San Diego (even the names are more revealing) than to the *variedad* cabarets in Tijuana. There are basically two types of girl-viewing bars in San Diego, "topless" and "naked". The topless bars are much more what I think Mexican men would prefer. Young women with no body fat and unusual chest development dance wearing only a *tanga* (or what they would call, for some reason, a "G-string").

"The atmosphere is noisy and festive. College boys, sailors, *mexicanos* and Asian men: they all act like boys first exposed to the exposed. They yell and cheer, they slop beers, they loudly worship at the altar of the unfettered breast. Oddly, I find them more degrading to women than the "naked" bars, in which women dance naked on a stage and men sit and watch. After the dance, the men leave money on the stage and the girls, now somewhat dressed, go around and pick up the tips, smiling and thanking the men, who offer compliments. I have been told that San Diego is a very strict and puritanical town, that in other American cities I would see less tame entertainment, often involving contact with the dancers. The "lap dance", the "couch dance" are evocative terms. And start to take the discussion away from showing flesh to performing sex acts. For that, a man would prefer the Tijuana clubs to those of California. But what I have been talking about is not prostitution, but *variedad* — woman as visual spectacle. And in that realm, there is no comparison between the *cantinas* and the "titty bars".

Since I am not a man, I suppose I should explain my familiarity with San Diego emporiums such as The Body Shop, Les Girls and Déjà vu, and my implied knowledge of Mexican show bars. It was for journalistic reasons—a *disculpa* which has dressed up many indiscretions in my career—and to balance an article I wrote earlier in my career. It may be rare for a "nice Mexican woman" like myself to be in "places like that" in California or Nevada, but less rare than for a decent Mexicana to set foot in a Mexican *cantina* of the *variedad* sort.

Cantinas are always screened from the street, so women generally have no idea what goes on inside. Of course we can imagine, but imagination very often embellishes reality (a principle widely applied inside the cabarets). Women of the non-professional type are not allowed in cantinas and none of the self-respecting type would allow themselves to be taken to *var-iedad* places, so these haunts of men present women with a sort of cultural black hole.

As a younger woman, very taken by my newfound role as social investigator, I was delighted to plunge into that hole, the better to emerge with the facts for the advancement of womankind. I wrote an article about such places for "¡*Hembrazo!*", a radical feminist magazine that has not survived. I would not think of myself as a radical nor a feminist; only as curious. I was admitted to the dark shadows of the bars easily: I disguised myself as a prostitute. It was a simple disguise: mostly short skirts, obvious jewelry and lots of underwear worn outside—much the same as the current fashions among Tijuana prostitutes and stylish American girls. The disguise allowed me to pass into those sanctuaries but brought me few offers of cash business, for which I never knew whether to be thankful or resentful. As well as helping me get the story—exploration of a previously unknown habitat—that turned out to be somewhat disappointing. The article was slightly notorious, by the way. More talked about than read, but with the result that several women would no longer speak to me and quite a few men no longer knew what to say to me.

I had anticipated my investigations revealing an atmosphere of free-wheeling sin. Casual carnality and a crude complicity. Instead, those caves of male sin turned out to be full of men sitting around drinking, listening to songs about men being betrayed by women they worshiped, and talking trivialities. There were prostitutes present, and occasionally a man would paw someone's breasts or follow someone's buttocks upstairs; but mostly the women are just furniture in a sort of boy's clubhouse, like the preserved heads and pelts of wild animals. The idea is a sort of lair where men can be men, a Neverland cave for lost boys. Ideally such lodges would be decorated with the skins and skulls of wolves, with the souvenirs of battle, with the paraphernalia of fast horses and cars, with naked women in chains. The more expensive and powerful the cave, the more closely those symbols resemble the real things they symbolize, become more potent totems. The ambiance of cantinas has remained the same since Revolutionary times.

To me the most interesting feature of the *variedad* club is its ordinariness. Even the women frequently seem no more exciting than those to whom these men must be married. Young women (and not so young) dance listlessly, making no eye contact, wearing bikinis and extremely high heels. Commonly they never really reveal anything you would not see on any beach, but the men stare and applaud. I found myself wondering if there was some sort of hypnosis in effect: that certain things, if presented in a *risqué* atmosphere, suddenly become sexually charged or possessed of a branded allure.

Sometimes you can watch act after act—and there is very little of what you would call variety in the usual sense of the word—before seeing any actual nudity. A girl might suddenly pull up her bra or tug down her panties for the last few bars of a song before the lights go down. I've seen girls drop their panties around their ankles to shuffle around in their *distante* heels like a little girl going to the bathroom—a sight that might be more vulnerable and arousing than any naked stripper laying wide open to lustful eyes. But such glimpses can be rare and only momentary.

Even stranger to me are the "featured acts", *"artistas"* breathlessly announced by the jaded masters of ceremony, who enter and leave to great applause. And what do these stars of the variety circuit offer? They are generally fleshy *quarentonas* (in Mexico there's a word for women in our forties) no more attractive than I am. They wear sequined costumes and many coats of makeup and have, to me, that sad air of circus performers seen close up. They strut in the spotlights and don't really strip, don't even sing, just lip-synch—what we would call *pleybak*. I could have done it myself, certainly more successfully than my whore impersonation. These *vedettes* are no younger than I am, no slimmer, no prettier, and probably don't sing any worse. What talent do they possess? Why are they billed as *artistas*? It might be relations with booking agents and impresarios. Perhaps they are playing out the last dregs of youthful stardom. But then where are the young ones? It could be that in Mexico it is possible to be a star of the sin circuit just by being willing to do it. Still, I have never understood. Here at the border, these shows are less common than in the interior, but they can be seen.

Another difference between the frontier and the interior is the new clubs that feature American girls doing American shows at American prices. They use booming rock or rap music and beautiful blond gringas do an extremely sexy show with absolutely no *Mexicana* inhibitions. Including bouncing around on customer's laps for twenty dollars: twice what many girls on the street charge to go to a hotel with customers. The full contact dance seems more efficient to me, and certainly medically safer. On *Avenida Revolución* this new type of dancing—called *teibol*—has pushed out the old *variedad* shows, though they survive down in the traditional red zone, the Cuahuila. The new places are nothing like cantinas: they are chrome and neon, cold and dark and sleek. They provide no haven for men, just access to women.

Which may be precisely what men go to cantinas to avoid. It is only through contact with American men that I have realized something about Mexican men: they are uncomfortable with women. It is almost as though there are two worlds that only meet in certain uneasy spots. The women and children group up—usually in the kitchen—and the men are all in a cantina somewhere. Or in a new suburban version, the men are all outside standing around a pickup truck, listening to its tape player and drinking beer. The men lavish attention when attempting a conquest, and are distinctly on edge being around single women on whom their attempts have not born fruit. Among themselves they seem relaxed enough, but the presence of women quickly changes that. Except prostitutes: they can ignore them because conquest is not an issue and once they are known, there are better things on which to spend money—like drinking with other men. Even in American bars that specialize in televised sports, women can enter if they like without making the men nervous. In fact, some women turn out to be fans of the games and watch them with the men and are tolerated in discussions if they know what they are talking about. And why not? Any woman who understands the complexities of American football deserves a perverse respect.

Mexican men tend to treat "professional" women with a calm, "keep your shirt on" type of impassivity, yet lose all perspective in the face of potentially available "amateurs". On the other hand American men get very excited about prostitutes, at least in Tijuana, and the idea that dancers can be had for more personal forms of expression, yet treat single women not working in the field with a cool reserve. Perhaps this is because in the United States it is evidently possible for talk with women to turn out later to have been illegal. But then, male-only cantinas are also illegal there.

All of which is merely a comparison of what I have seen of the two cultures (American and Mexican, that is—I don't think I can get a perspective on the Male/Female cultural divide, though I am trying). To return to my explorations of what goes on behind the shadowy doors that hide our men away, my impressions were not so much disappointing as somewhat saddening. Among the sin is a sort of innocence that seems to stem from solitude. Strangely, it was in many of the places that swarm with prostitutes, places of assignation with the actual beds upstairs or in the rear, that I felt that innocence most strongly. I saw a great many middle-aged men sitting at tables talking to women. They would drink, be courtly or macho, bathe in the female attention. In a way I sensed that they are looking for a woman that could be talked to without losing their maleness, who is a woman sexually but really one of their *cuates*, one of the guys. They can get sex at home from their wives: what they look for in prostitutes is company.

And, of course, attention. Especially, attention to vanity. Pretty young women treat them as if they are attractive, compliment them with their company. I have heard of clubs in Los Angeles where men pay just to dance with girls, to talk and drink with them. It is the fashion for women to laugh at that, to object to it. Yet I have seen women pay terrible prices just to dance and talk and drink with men. The things men seek are different from what we women want, but not that far apart. I came to see the cantinas as something other than dins of sin. Well, actual sinning may take place there, but more important is the air of it, the symbols and attitudes of experienced sinners.

If women recoil from that, perhaps we should all ask ourselves the question that occurred to me during my investigation: What is the female equivalent of all this? We should examine our own caves, our own magazines full of advertisements for "daring" and "sensual", the language of fashion. We could just walk into Dorians and start reading the names of perfumes. I recently bought a cheaper scent that promises to resemble "My Sin" so closely that the difference would not be noticed within lethal range. To tell the truth (a truth not accepted by the feminist editors of "¡*Hembrazo*!") do you know what I was most reminded of in the public privacy of all those dark cantinas? Beauty parlors. They are male retreats, different from female retreats because men are different from women. But what is happening? People are spending time and money to be told they are attractive. People are paying money to have their hands held, to share gossip, to participate in rituals and values they inherited from their parents. People are taking an indulgence, a vacation from the other sex. Except members of that sex who behave in the right way.

I came to see the *muchachas* stroking the men in those dark male "caves" as a version the elegant homosexual hairdressers I have seen in expensive female "boudoirs". Men like my ex-husband come in and spend a hundred dollars to sit around and talk, feel masculine and be artificially fussed over by pretty young women: my friends spend more money than that to sit around, feel feminine, and be fussed over by pretty young artificial men. To each according to their taste, from each according to their means.

The saddest result of my article, for me personally, was that I started to understand my ex-husband. I could see a little of what he wanted—and in fact can't we, the women, have the charity to say "needed"? And that I had not given it to him. Maybe it was my failure for not having it to give, maybe his for not being able to ask, maybe it was more the case that we were both trained to be unable to be company to each other. When he wanted company, did he get it from me; or only talk about children and housework and recipes? When he wanted someone to admire his masculinity did he only get responsibility? In understanding him, I start to understand myself a little, which is what journalism was supposed to be about in the first place. Not that I'd ever go back to that pig. But I have wondered at times, what investigations he would have to undertake to start to understand my needs.

About the Authors . . .

Linton Robinson is a veteran freelance writer, experienced border watcher, and author of *Mexican Slang 101.*

Ana Maria Corona Espinosa is the pen name of a Tijuana writer. She is a single mother of three who moved from her native Guadalajara to Tijuana, where she regards two countries with detached concern.

About the Artist . . .

Victor Cauduro Rojas, the cover artist, is considered one of Mexico's finest younger painters. His remarkable work and career are displayed at:

ww.victorcauduro.com